A Rare Gift

Crystal Journals: Book 1

G. ROSEMARY LUDLOW

This is a work of fiction. All of the characters, organizations, and events portrayed in this novel are either the products of the author's imagination or are used fictitiously.

1. Juvenile Fiction 2. Historical 3. United States 4. 19th Century

Summary: When a young girl is given a crystal that takes her back in time, she discovers adventure and danger unlike anything she's ever experienced in her safe, predictable world.

Cover Design by Diogo Lando

Library and Archives Canada Cataloguing in Publication

ISBN-13: 9780973687118
ISBN-10: 0973687118
Published by: Comwave Publishing House Inc.2751 Oxford Street, Vancouver, BC V5K 1N5

For Lock

My Rock. My Shoulder. My Ideas Man

ACKNOWLEDGEMENTS

So many people contribute to the creation of a book.

I start by thanking Kit Pearson who first showed me that what I wrote was worthwhile.

And then, of course, our wonderful writing group, Jen Jensen, Irene Watts, and Russell Kelly. We pushed each other to do better.

Lately, I must thank Shauna Pratt, and Alex L'Allier for incisive read-throughs and Leisl Kaberry and the Create Space Team for hand-holding me through the publishing process.

Thanks also go to the monumentally patient Diogo Lando, who created my book cover.

CONTENTS

1

A RARE GIFT

At ten years old, Susan was tall for her age. "Tall and willowy," her dad said. Her eyes were blue, and that was OK.

But her hair. Susan's hair was a "nothing" brown.

"Golden highlights," her mum said.

"Boring," Susan said.

It wasn't curly; it wasn't straight. It just waved all over the place. And so Susan made sure it was always cut short.

Whether she liked it or not, Susan was at the local flea market—again. *Every* Sunday morning her parents dragged her along with them. It was boring. Susan was annoyed. She kicked at a clump of grass. It didn't move. Susan kicked it again. Now she had a dirty shoe.

The flea market was in a large field just off the freeway. All summer people came from cities, towns, and villages across Vancouver Island to buy and sell their wares. It was a meeting place for neighbors—and strangers.

It was a pleasant ritual for Susan's parents. As soon as they arrived, Mr. and Mrs. Sinclair busied themselves setting up their table. They came often and knew everyone. People hurried over to see Mrs. Sinclair's latest carvings.

Mostly, Mrs. Sinclair brought her small pieces to the market. "Tactiles," she called them. Small pieces of stone, smooth in some places and rough in others. People liked to hold them in their hands and run their fingers along the grooves. Sometimes she brought little animals she had carved.

Soon her parents were chatting and laughing with their neighbors.

Susan wandered away to the end of a row.

There she noticed an old lady standing quietly. Susan had never seen her at the market before. She didn't seem to be part of all the busyness. She looked ancient. Her gray hair curled around her face. Her skin looked wrinkled and lined. And yet, the lady stood tall and straight. Her hands on her hips. A smile on her face.

A cat sat on the table. A gray tabby, watching the people passing by. Too aloof. A cat just like Puddy. Susan stretched out her hand. The cat half closed its eyes, watching her. Just the tip of its neatly placed tail moved.

Susan pulled her hand back. This cat looked like Puddy, but Puddy had died. Susan could not remember a time without Puddy, until now. It was old age. Puddy got slower and slower, until he stopped. Susan really missed Puddy.

The not-Puddy cat stood, stretched, and leaped from the table. It rubbed itself once against the lady's legs and then wandered off to explore.

Susan glanced at the lady and saw that the lady was watching her. Just like the cat.

Susan turned away, but before she took a step, she noticed the basket that stood in the middle of the lady's table.

Everywhere else tables were laden with piles of knick-knacks and interesting junk, but just one large basket sat in the middle of the old lady's table.

Hmmm, different. Susan edged closer to see what was in the basket.

Filling it about halfway were polished stones and colored crystals. Just that.

Maybe this is where Judy got her crystal, Susan thought. Her best friend, Judy, had a crystal, and she had gone on and on about its healing powers; and how wonderful it was to have a crystal; and how everyone should have a crystal; and why didn't Susan have a crystal? *I'm starting to think like Judy*, Susan thought.

She slipped a bit closer. The old lady wiped the table with a cloth. Susan leaned over and peeped into the basket. It wouldn't do to seem *too* interested. The lady just kept wiping the table.

Susan was surprised at how pretty and sparkly the crystals looked. They were all jumbled together with the polished stones in the basket. Reds, blues, greens, even a lovely purple one. Susan reached forward. She liked the look of the purple one. Judy had a red one, but Susan admired the way the purple crystal caught the light. She looked at the lady, and the lady looked at her.

Quickly she pulled her hand back. "Um," she said, "how much are they?"

"A dollar each." The lady didn't smile. She seemed very uninterested.

Susan had a dollar.

"I'd like the purple one, please."

The lady shrugged. "You pick it out. There are other purple ones underneath you might like better. You can stick your hand in if you want to."

Susan used her finger to stir the stones in the basket. They felt cool and smooth against her skin and made a rattling sound as she moved them. She noticed a clear crystal lying among the others. It was not colored, it was not large, and it was not bright, but when Susan touched it, she felt a tingle. She pulled her hand away.

She looked deep into the basket, but could no longer see the one that had tingled her finger. She thrust her hand into the basket. There it was again. She pulled out her hand, and the tingly crystal nestled in her palm.

"You're sure that's the one you want?" the old woman snapped at Susan.

Susan shook her head vigorously. No, she wanted the purple one. "I have a dollar." Susan bit her lip. *What am I saying?*

"It's very ordinary," the woman said. "Here, wouldn't you rather have this beautiful purple one?" The woman held out a large, square purple stone. She moved it in her hand so it glinted in the sunlight.

Susan reached out to the purple crystal, but didn't touch it. "It's beautiful," she said. Susan meant to put the clear crystal back in the basket, but for some reason she gripped it tighter in her hand. "I want this one," she heard herself say. *What did I just say? What is happening to me?*

Susan threw the crystal back into the basket. She swirled all the stones around, and selected a crystal at random. The clear crystal was in her hand again. She put it on the tabletop and poked her hand into the basket. She selected a crystal. She looked at her choice. It was the clear crystal again. Her hand tingled.

The woman's face broke into a huge grin. "It seems to be yours," she said. "You shall have it." The woman threw the purple one back into the basket. She rested her hands on her ample hips and beamed down at Susan.

Susan dropped her money on the table, but the woman scooped it up and thrust it back into her hand. "*That* crystal is free." she said.

"Free?"

"It's a gift." The woman nodded.

Susan opened her hand to look at the crystal—her crystal. It was six sided and tapered to a point at one end. Well, not exactly a point. Susan had never seen a crystal like it before. It nestled in the palm of her hand as though it were made for it.

"Thank you very much," Susan said without taking her eyes from the crystal.

"You're very welcome." The woman bowed a little toward Susan. "Now, I need to explain to you why the crystal is special."

All of Susan's attention focused on the crystal. Why was it special? It felt special, but looking at it closely, it could have been a piece of glass. Susan took a step.

It stuck to my hand, she thought. *Why did it do that?* Susan took another step.

"Now I must tell you," the woman said.

But Susan didn't listen. She took another step away.

"Wait. Wait." The woman waved her arm and made a grab at Susan's arm.

But Susan didn't wait. She wandered off into the crowd with most of her attention on the crystal in her hand.

Susan ignored the other flea market tables; she stepped through the jostling, bustling crowd. She walked back to the family van. It was locked, so she lay on the grass in the warm summer sun. The crystal caught the sunlight and seemed to glow from inside. Susan watched the glints and glitter as she moved the crystal in her palm. Her head drooped onto her arms, and then her eyes closed and Susan fell asleep.

2

IT BEGINS

"Come on now, laddie, y' can't be sleepin' 'ere."

Susan awoke, startled. Someone was roughly shaking her shoulder.

"Wh…wa…" Susan blinked the sleep from her eyes. She tried to make sense of what she could see.

She was on a ship, a wooden one. She could see huge sails filled with wind over the shoulder of the sailor shaking her. He waved a hook in her face, and he smelled of salt and tar. The hook was where his hand should be.

"Get up now, I tell ye." The sailor used his hook to haul her to her feet. The hook felt hard and sharp through her sweatshirt.

"Ye can't be sleepin' in the gangway, or it's a beatin' you'll be gettin', lad." The sailor pushed her out onto the wooden deck.

She tripped and stumbled over bundles and boxes until she found her footing. Trembling and uncertain, she looked for a new place to settle among the many people thronging the deck. She needed time to think.

She remembered waiting by the family van at the flea market. She remembered feeling sleepy. She had never had a dream this real before. Susan looked around. She recognized no one. She peered at the faces. Everyone wore very old-fashioned clothing. No one wore jeans—nobody else had a sweatshirt. All the jackets she saw were rough wool in dark colors. All the women wore long, full skirts, and many had shawls wrapped around their shoulders. They looked thin and hungry, and their clothes were old and frayed.

A few children played tag around and through the boxes and bundles. When the ship pitched and rolled in the waves, most lost their balance. They skidded across the deck, bumping into the adults who stood or sat around in groups.

Farther down the deck, Susan saw a large boy chasing a shorter one. By the look on their faces, she knew they were not playing. The large boy made a huge lunge, but the small boy was agile and ducked under the other's grasping arms. He dashed in Susan's direction, skidded on a slippery spot, and banged into the mast she was leaning against. *Crack*. His head hit the solid wood. The larger boy turned away, trying to look as though he had not caused the fall.

Susan turned her attention to the boy sprawled at her feet. He was very thin. He wore a ragged sweater over a frayed shirt. The sweater was unraveling at the cuffs. His hair was a sandy color, too long, and it bristled everywhere. His nose was straight and looked red and sore from too much sun. She hoped he was all right. She was just about to reach out and shake him when his eyes opened. They were a bright green.

"What are you staring at?" he sneered, pulling himself up.

"Are you OK?"

"You're with Slade, you are."

"Slade?" Susan was puzzled.

"Trying to steal my knife, you were."

Susan couldn't believe this rude person. "I wasn't stealing your knife," she said. "I just wanted to know if you were all right."

"Think you're pretty posh for a boy in funny clothes, don't ya?" The boy jeered at her, reaching over and poking her sweatshirt.

"You think *my* clothes are funny?" Susan stood up with hands on hips and glared down at the boy. "You look like you escaped from a movie set."

The boy stood up, too. A little knife appeared in his hand, and he began to spin it round in his fingers.

"You shan't have my knife. It's my knife, and I'm going to keep it."

It looks like a fruit knife, Susan thought. The boy seemed to think it was a weapon.

I'll show you," he yelled, and he sprang at Susan with the knife out.

"Hey—a!" Without even thinking, Susan applied all she had learned at kung fu class. *Use his momentum against him,* an inner voice reminded her. The stance, the grip, the move…she had the knife, and the puny boy was spinning across the deck again. He looked very surprised.

Susan was surprised, too. Her parents insisted that she take the classes. "It will give you confidence," they argued. Driving into town every Saturday morning for months was not her idea of a good time, but now she could see the use of all the stepping and posing and kicking. *Maybe I'll go again in the fall,* she thought.

The boy lay on the deck, panting. None of the adults took any notice.

Susan looked at the knife in her hands. Just a small knife—the blade no longer than three inches. The handle was creamy-colored bone. A whale was carved on it. The whale was black and sticking way up out of the sea. It was spouting a fountain of water, rather than just the small spurt that came from a real whale.

"I better go and see if he's all right," she muttered and started toward him.

Seeing her coming, the boy jumped up and, glaring at her, slipped between two groups of adults.

I'll watch for him, Susan thought as she slipped the knife into her back pocket. She looked around to find a quieter place to sit.

She saw the old woman. The old woman from the flea market.

A friendly face. At first, on seeing her, Susan felt relief. But then......*Have I been kidnapped? Was I drugged? How did I get here?* Susan ducked behind a box and watched.

The woman was sitting on several huge bundles tied in bright-colored cloth. She was looking around at everything.

She looks a little sad, Susan noticed.

I can't just hide here forever, I have to know what's happening. Susan stood.

The woman beckoned her over.

"What's happening?" Susan blurted out.

The old woman looked at her sideways. Even though she smiled, Susan thought her eyes looked sad. The old woman patted the bundle next to her, inviting Susan to sit.

Susan sighed and sat. She turned to the woman and waited for an explanation. The woman seemed to be gathering her thoughts.

"Where am I?" Susan asked. "Why do they all think I'm a boy?"

"Ah." The woman chuckled. "Two important questions. Get comfortable, and I'll explain."

Susan wriggled into the bundles to make a hollow, but her eyes never left the old woman's face.

"You're in the past; the year is about 1864," the old woman said. "They think you're a boy because your hair is short, and you are wearing jeans. In this time women never wear trousers."

"Not ever?" Susan shook her head.

"You're on a sailing ship, crossing the Atlantic Ocean to New York in America," the old woman continued. She waved her hand to indicate the people standing around. "These are immigrants going to America to try to build a better life for themselves and their families."

"How do you know?"

The woman laughed. "Oh, I've had some experience at this," she said. "You've been called to help. It's an adventure. It happens to a very few lucky people."

"This is lucky?" Susan's eyes scanned the decks. "This doesn't look lucky to me."

Her companion smiled. "Ah, but you're young yet."

Yes, I'm young, but I'm not stupid. Susan thought. *Adventures have swords and wizards and magic. This place smells. It's all a bit weird.*

"Well, OK, I've had the adventure." Susan tugged the lady's sleeve. "I want to go home now."

The woman smiled and patted her hand. "You've only just begun your first crystal journey," she said.

"Crystal journey?"

Susan remembered the crystal and reached into her pocket to pull it out.

"Oh, don't." The woman tried to catch her hand.

It was too late. As soon as Susan's hand grasped the crystal, the world began to swirl around her. The colors ran together into a white-light rainbow, and the noises all melded into one high note. The last thing she heard was the woman's voice saying, "It's a rare gift."

3

IT WAS A DREAM!

Susan sat up with a start.

She was in the grass beside the van.

"There you are, Susie Two Shoes." Her father walked around to the passenger door. "We've been looking for you."

Susan gulped for air. "I've been asleep—I think." She shook her head to clear it. She scurried into the back of the van as soon as the door was unlocked.

As they drove out of the parking lot across the ruts to the road, she took the crystal from her pocket and stared at it. It looked very ordinary. As she put her attention on it, though, it seemed to pull in the colors around it and reflect them at her. In her hand it looked ordinary, but for just a second, she remembered how it had stuck to her fingers.

"It's a rare gift," she said, puzzled, and thrust it deep into her pocket.

■ ■ ■

That night she put the crystal on her dresser and stroked it with her finger. It looked quite beautiful to her, even though it was simpler than the one her friend Judy had.

While she watched, the crystal gathered the light from her bedside lamp and pulled it into itself, and then the light glowed back out at her. Susan blinked and shook her head.

This is silly, she thought. *It's just a crystal, an ordinary crystal.* She ignored the fact that a very unusual woman had given her the crystal. Ignored the fact that the same woman appeared on the sailing ship in her dream. She ignored being told it was a rare gift. She even ignored the pitch and roll of the ship, which she still felt in her legs.

"I had a dream," she said emphatically to her reflection in the mirror. She winked. She nodded, and her reflection bobbed back at her. Susan climbed into bed and switched off the light.

■ ■ ■

The next morning Susan saw her crystal as soon as she opened her eyes. It stood on the dresser in exactly the place she had left it. The morning sun, shining through her window, caught in the crystal and broke into patches of bright colors that shone on the wall. The room was ablaze with tiny rainbows.

Susan jumped out of bed and moved her hands through the colored bands. Her hands took on the colors of violet, blue, yellow, orange as the pattern from the wall repeated on her hand. What a beautiful surprise! Susan was so glad to have the crystal. She picked it up to examine closely, and as she did, all the tiny rainbows in the room began to dance across the walls, the ceiling, and the floor. *It's like a laser light show,* she thought, laying the crystal down on the dresser again. She hurried off to the shower.

Her father was already at the table eating his toast when she bounced into the kitchen. He was reading the newspaper but looked up in surprise when she came bustling in.

"Why are you up so early, Suzie Blue Glue?"

"Good morning." Susan laughed, popping bread into the toaster. "Isn't it a beautiful morning?"

"Yes, it is," said her father dryly, "but that's never got you up so early before. What's happening?"

Susan almost told him about the crystal. She opened her mouth to begin, but at that moment, her mother arrived in the kitchen.

"Well, I see you two are making out OK," Mum commented as she poured herself coffee from the machine.

Over breakfast, her parents planned a shopping trip into town.

"Can you be ready in thirty minutes, Susan?"

"No, thanks." Susan definitely did not want to take the long drive into town. "I have to go see Judy after breakfast," she said.

■ ■ ■

Susan left at the same time as her parents. She waved to them as they drove away and then turned her bike toward Judy's house. After the first hill, she could usually coast all the way. Coming home was harder.

As she pedaled up the hill, she could feel the crystal in her pocket. Every time she pumped with her right leg, she was conscious of the lump it made against her thigh. Thinking of the crystal made her think about the poor, puny boy on the deck of the sailing ship. *It was only a dream,* she reminded herself forcefully.

"It was only a dream," she repeated over and over to the rhythm of her pedaling. But thoughts of the boy kept sneaking around the edges of her determination. The more she tried to push his image away, the more he settled into her thoughts.

On the whizzing descent to Judy's house, she yelled at the top of her lungs, "It was only a dream!"

Like an echo she heard, "It's a rare gift," quiet and close to her ear.

Judy's dog, Mutt, barked and jumped up, trying to nip the front wheel of her bike. Susan jumped off her bike and ruffled the fur around his neck. Mutt loved that. Mutt slurped her face in appreciation just as Judy ran into the yard to greet her. Susan didn't have to think about dreams or gifts, boys or knives anymore.

4

CRYSTALS

Judy had been in the city for a couple of days visiting her cousins. Judy had blond curly hair, lighter than Susan's. She had startling dark eyebrows and vivid blue eyes. Susan thought she was very pretty. Judy was short and stocky and played tennis, basketball, and softball. Susan sometimes went to games and cheered Judy on.

They sat on the swing seat in Judy's garden. Judy talked on and on about all her cousins; and what they were doing; and where they all went; and what games they had gone to. Baseball was the favorite at the moment.

Judy talked, and Susan listened. Each kicked off with a foot to keep the seat gently swinging. The chains made a soft creaking noise.

The sound reminded Susan of the noise the ropes made on the ship when a powerful gust of wind billowed the sails. She pushed the thought away. *It was only a dream*, she reminded herself.

Susan pulled out her crystal and held it up for Judy.

"Oh, Sue Sue, it's so bright! Where did you get it? Mine isn't nearly as bright as yours. Mine has the same number of facets, but it's a different shape. Mine is bigger than yours. See?" Judy pulled her crystal out of her T-shirt and dangled it under Susan's nose. Judy's had a chain attached, and she always wore it around her neck. Judy knew a lot about crystals.

Without pausing, Judy went on, "How much did you pay for it? Not too much, I bet. Did you get a card with it?"

Susan wanted to tell Judy about the unusual lady, but Judy went straight on. "Mine had a card, and it said it had magical properties and would keep me healthy, but I still got a cold last winter, but it didn't last as long."

Susan often wondered how Judy found time to breathe. She always talked nonstop like this—Susan was used to it.

Judy chattered on, but Susan's attention zeroed in on the light in her crystal. She could see light right inside. It glowed back at her. Not the rainbow light of this morning, but a steady, warm glow that made her feel very safe.

"...come on, I'll show you." Judy pulled her arm and stood up.

Susan jumped, realizing she had missed more of the conversation than she should have. She stood and followed Judy into the house. Usually if she just went along, she caught up with what was happening. Judy marched her down the passage toward Darren's bedroom.

Surely not there. Susan preferred to avoid everything to do with Judy's brother.

The door was plastered with a huge poster of an army tank with the gun pointing straight out into the hallway. Underneath Darren had written a sign.

KEEP OUT—THIS MEANS YOU—TRESPASS AT RISK OF YOUR LIFE.

Judy opened the door casually and strode into the room.

"He had to go into town," she explained. Nevertheless, she shut the door very quietly.

"I told you." Judy moved over to his desk under the window. "See," she said, pointing, "he's growing crystals."

Susan hurried over. "Growing crystals? They aren't plants, are they?"

"No, silly." Judy laughed. "I told you. They're minerals, and they all gather together and make crystals. They grow, see?" She pointed to a saucer on the desk by the window. "There's one he started yesterday, and this one will grow bigger now."

Susan saw a saucer filled with yellow liquid. A rock stood in the middle, and delicate slivers of crystal clung to it. Also on the desk stood a large jar. Susan peered in. It was two-thirds full of blue liquid, and hanging down from the top of the jar, on a string, was a little crystal. Susan could see it suspended in the liquid. This crystal was a lot bigger than the ones in the saucer.

"Darren explained it," Judy said. "You dissolve the minerals in water and then give them a place to cling to, and they form these crystals." Judy waved her hand at the jar. "That little crystal hanging there will give a clinging place for the minerals in the liquid. It will get bigger than it is now. It happens in nature, too, and it's how we got our crystals. Sometimes in laboratories they can grow really big ones, but they're always flawed—they have little imperfections in them..."

Susan tuned Judy out. She stared at these beautiful, tiny crystals. She had had no idea they were so interesting. She thought crystals were just the latest fad at school. She let Judy drag her out of the room, down the passage, and into her own bedroom.

Judy was still talking.

Susan plomped down on the bed.

"If you have a magnifying glass, you can sometimes see the flaw." Judy joined her. "Here I'll show you mine." Judy hauled out the huge magnifying glass she had bought when she was interested in butterflies, and began to peer closely at her crystal.

"It's here somewhere," she muttered. "Yes, there it is." She held the crystal right under Susan's nose. Susan took the magnifying glass and peered at Judy's crystal. She could see a place where it looked slightly cracked.

She looked up. "Is the crack the flaw?"

"Uh-huh." Judy nodded. "Now let's find yours."

Susan didn't want to let go of her crystal. She held it on her palm and braced with the other hand to keep it still. Judy peered closely at it through the glass.

"Turn it over, Sue Sue." Judy sounded surprised. "I can't see a flaw anywhere on that side."

Susan turned it over and over again. They both looked, but they could not find a flaw anywhere within the crystal.

"Well, it must be there." Judy was positive. "Darren told me they have to go into outer space to make perfect crystals. I guess it's just very small. I'm hungry. Let's see what's to eat." Without waiting for a reply, Judy hurried down the hall and into the kitchen.

Susan heard her opening the fridge, then banging the bread board, but she took the time to check over her crystal one more time. She still could see no flaw in it anywhere.

Carefully she thrust it into her pocket and hurried to the kitchen. Judy often made very weird sandwiches, and Susan didn't feel like sardines and peanut butter today.

5

IT WAS NO DREAM

As Susan walked her bike up the path to home, her head span with new knowledge about crystals and new wonder at her "rare gift."

Every step of the walk brought her mental images of the puny boy on the heaving deck of a sailing ship, coming to America. In her mind's eye, she could see his face and his threadbare sweater unravelling in the brisk sea wind. Remembering the way his fingers moved over the knife made her fingers twitch on her handle bars. The way she had taken it away from him made her smile. The whole experience seemed so real. *It was only a dream,* she reassured herself.

"It was only a dream. It was only a dream."

She kept saying it but still felt connected to the boy in some weird way.

■ ■ ■

Her mother was hanging washing on the line when Susan wheeled her bike around the corner. She stayed to help. They chatted and laughed and struggled to get the damp sheets spread on the line in the brisk wind.

Life seemed so normal. *It's silly to let one dream set my whole life on edge,* she decided. *The crystal in my pocket is just a crystal. Just a crystal.*

■ ■ ■

Susan went up to bed at nine o'clock. She turned on the light and went straight to the dresser to brush her hair out, but she did not reach for her brush. There, on the smooth polished top of her dresser, was the nasty boy's knife.

6

GIVE IT BACK

Susan hesitantly reached out her hand. She poked the knife with her finger. Yes, it was real. She picked it up and examined it closely. It certainly looked like the knife she had taken from the boy. She could see the black whale against the creamy color of the bone. In her dream, she had slipped it into her back pocket.

Susan sank down on the bed, knife in hand. She couldn't think anymore.

She was still sitting there when her mother came to say good night.

"Ah, Susan, I see you have the knife," she said. "I've told you before, turn out your pockets before you throw your clothes in the hamper." She sat next to Susan. "You're lucky I didn't put it through the wash." She lifted a strand of Susan's hair back to get her attention. "I don't like you carrying a knife, Susan. Where did you get it? It looks very old."

These questions shook Susan out of her shock. She didn't want to tell a lie, but she didn't know the truth.

Finally she stammered out something about getting it from a boy and she had forgotten she still had it.

Susan's mum pulled her hair back into a little ponytail. "Maybe we could start with it like that," she said.

"Oh, Mum." Susan pulled it out and fluffed up her hair. "I like it short. You know that."

"Well, at least you have my nice, straight nose and my nice, fine eyebrows." Mum laughed. "Imagine if you had bushy eyebrows like your dad."

"Yes, but I do have the Sinclair figure—you always say." Susan laughed, too. This naming of what she looked like was an old joke between Susan and her mother.

"Good night," her mother said as she bent over and kissed her forehead. At the door she turned. "I want you to give the knife back tomorrow," she said and switched off the light.

■ ■ ■

Susan lay in the dark. Give it back. She would be happy to. She wished she had never seen the knife! Dream knives did not appear on your dresser. She had read a lot of books, and this is what happened there—in books. *There must be another explanation*, she thought as she turned over and pulled the covers more securely around her shoulders.

Her crystal was the last thing she saw before she closed her eyes. It gathered light from somewhere and glowed softly. She saw the knife next to it, illuminated by the glow.

I wish it was only a dream, she thought.

Eventually, she sighed and slipped into a deep sleep.

7

THE SAILING SHIP

Pain. Her hair. Someone was pulling her hair! Susan woke
with a start. She opened her eyes—then she wanted to close
them again. The puny boy stood too close and looked very
angry. She was back in her dream, and it hurt.

He jammed his face up against hers and held her close.
He yanked her hair again. Susan tried to wriggle free, but
he held her tightly.

"I'll fix you," he yelled. "Where's my knife?" He pulled
her onto her feet by the hair.

That was his mistake. When she stood, Susan's feet
were free, and she kicked out at his knee and shins. Even
barefoot she connected hard. He let her go and limped off,
howling.

Susan looked around, hoping no one had noticed. She
pulled her clothes straight—and realized she was still in

her pajamas. She wanted to die. She was standing on a sailing ship, in a crowd of people, in a suit with teddy bears printed all over it. The teddy bears wore red bow ties, but she still didn't feel properly dressed.

She crept off to find a quiet place, her face as red as the bow ties.

The wind blew cold on the deck, and before she found an unoccupied sheltered spot, her whole body was covered in goose bumps. She huddled up into a small ball, drawing her knees to her chest. Crying would not help, but a tear slid down her cheek anyway, followed by another. She felt so lost.

It's night at home, she thought, *but it's day here. It's summer at home. Here, it feels like winter.* Susan shook her head. Another puzzle.

Susan tried to think back to her last experience on this deck. The crystal lady had been here. Maybe she was still on the ship and could explain what was happening. She crept out of her hiding place. Hopping and jumping and flapping her arms to keep warm, Susan circulated among the people, looking for the old woman.

She found the boy instead. He looked as cold, lost, and bedraggled as she was. He sat curled up in the lee of some boxes. He sniffed and wiped his face on his sleeve. Susan crept closer and noticed he was rubbing his shin with his free hand.

"Serves you right," she said, standing over him. "Teach you to pick on...me." She almost said "a girl" but remembered, just in time, that here she looked like a boy.

The boy turned around suddenly, shock on his face. Then with no hesitation at all, he howled and jumped at her. Susan was ready and jumped back out of his grasp. He grabbed again, but missed again.

"Give me back my knife," he yelled.

"I would"—Susan dodged again—"but I haven't got it with me."

"Liar." The boy shrank back on himself. Susan backed off, and the boy curled into an even tighter ball, out of the wind.

Susan continued her search for the old woman, but after a while, she had to admit the woman was not on the ship. She tried asking people, but no one had seen the woman Susan described. Cold from the wind and damp from the sea spray, Susan crept back to the cubby she had found. She didn't know what else to do.

She curled up into a tight ball as the boy had done. It kept what little heat she had close to her body. She thought about the boy. Such a nasty person. Always lashing out. And so ragged and dirty. What made a person behave like that?

Deep in thought, Susan didn't notice gentle rustling noises coming closer. Over the creak of the sails, she didn't hear the boy's feet scuffling on the deck.

"Give me my knife!" he yelled and pulled her from her cover by the arm. "I need my knife," he went on, shaking her where she lay. Susan grabbed at his knees. He tumbled on top of her, and the two of them rolled across the deck.

Sitting on her chest, he shook her shoulders, but Susan was distracted because, out of the corner of her eye, she could see her crystal lying against a box. *It's about the same distance from me now, as my bed is to my dresser.* Her thoughts bounced in her head to the rhythm of the shaking.

She reached her hand out; the shaking actually helped to move her closer. She stretched and strained. The crystal was at her fingertips. She stretched as far as she could, but then the boy bounced her by the shoulders, again, away from the crystal. She needed her crystal.

"I need my knife. Give me my knife," the boy went on.

"All right, all right," Susan chattered through the shaking. Anything to make him stop. Anything to reach the crystal. "Let me up, and I'll get it," she said.

The boy stopped. He eyed her suspiciously. Susan tried to look sincere. "I'll get it. I promise. I need to go home to get it. Let me up."

Slowly the boy eased his weight onto his knees. In a flash, she rolled over and grabbed the crystal into the safety of her grasp. Immediately, the world around her began to swirl. As everything smeared she heard one loud, anguished "no!" from the boy.

She felt dizzy, spinning; colors smeared; noises blurred. And then she heard the rustle of her bedsheets as she landed on her bed. The knife lay on the dresser. The boy was nowhere. Her shoulders ached. Susan stretched to get the stiffness out. She turned on the light. Her bedroom looked beautiful.

8

TAKE IT BACK

By breakfast time, and after a sleepless night, Susan had made up her mind. The crystal was going back to the lady. As Susan slathered peanut butter onto her toast, she couldn't believe her ears. Her mother and father were planning a trip to another flea market. *Maybe my luck is changing,* she thought.

"Can I come?" she asked, biting down on her toast.

Her parents exchanged a surprised look. Susan usually had to be dragged to a flea market.

Her mother shrugged. "We're leaving right after breakfast."

Susan jumped up, gulping the last of her milk, and rushed to her room.

"I have a couple of things to get," she said. "I'll be down in a minute."

In her room, she quickly put the crystal into a little jewelry pouch she had. It was brown velveteen with a gold silk cord. She pulled the cord very tight with a quick jerk. Just as she rushed from the room, she noticed the little knife. She grabbed it and pushed it into the pocket of her jeans. The brown pouch with the crystal followed it, and down the stairs she ran. Susan reached the van first for the trip.

"Aren't you the eager one?" Her father laughed as he loaded some old boxes into the back. "What's your hurry, Suzie Too Soon?"

Susan couldn't think of one good reason for her hurry that she could tell her father. She opened her mouth, not sure what would come out, but fortunately, her mother jumped into the van, and they were off. By the time the car reached the road and the gate was shut behind them, her father had forgotten his unanswered question.

This market was held in an old, disused drive-in movie theater. The screen was still half standing at one end. All the people laid out their tables and goods in lines across the area. Susan quickly slipped into the crowd. She knew which stall she was looking for. She wanted to find the woman and return the crystal as quickly as possible. She looked, but the woman could not be seen.

Then she noticed a box of polished pebbles under a table. It was in a jumble with boxes of books, an old sewing machine, and a black velvet painting.

I'll just drop it into the box, she thought, *and that will be the end of it.*

She reached into her pocket while she was sidling through the knickknacks toward the box. Suddenly a hand came down hard on her shoulder.

"Don't touch the crystal!" an urgent voice said right by her ear.

Susan whirled around and came face-to-face with the woman. The woman from the ship, the woman who had given her the crystal, the woman who had started all this mess she was in. Looking at her strong, pleasant, smiling face, Susan could feel her anger rising.

"Take it back," she demanded. "I hate it. My life's a mess. Take it back!"

The woman laughed and held up her hands in mock horror. "Such vehemence. It's a rare gift."

"A rare gift," Susan mimicked, and her voice rose with anger. "A rare gift. It's a nightmare. What did I ever do to you so you would give me this weird crystal?"

Then the woman sighed. She beckoned to Susan and then walked toward the trees bordering the area. "You are obviously upset. Let's go get a drink, and we'll talk about it."

"Talk. I don't want to talk. I just want to give you the crystal and get out of here." Susan grabbed the little velveteen bag from her pocket and held it out. "Here, take it," she said.

The woman shook her head. There was an amused look in her eyes. "I can't take it," she said.

Susan thrust the bag toward the woman. "Take it," she insisted.

The woman sighed again and shook her head. "Listen to me. I can't take it, and you can't give it away. It's yours. It chose you, and you chose it. Let me explain about it, and then you will understand."

But Susan still held the little velveteen bag out to the woman.

"OK." The woman shook her head in a resigned way and held out her hand. "I'll show you," she said. "Take it out of the bag and give it to me.

At last.

Susan hurried to obey. The silk cord was pulled tightly where she had jerked it. Finally the ties loosened, and she dropped the crystal into her open palm. The woman still had her hand out, and Susan reached to place the crystal in it. Her hand was moving very slowly. The harder Susan reached, the slower her hand went. It was like pushing her hand into a pillow.

Susan relaxed her arm and drew the crystal back to her body. Quickly she moved as if to throw it into the woman's outstretched hand. She made the whole movement, but for some reason, the crystal never left her hand.

Susan tried other ways to transfer the crystal from her hand to the woman's, but none of them worked. She kept trying. The woman waited, not speaking.

Finally, Susan knew without question the crystal was hers.

"I can't," she said, looking into the woman's eyes for the first time. She saw amusement there still, but she also saw understanding and a certain sadness. Susan saw that the woman would be happy to have the crystal back if she could. With that realization, the last of Susan's resistance woofed out of her. Slowly and deliberately she returned the crystal to the bag and put it back into her pocket.

She didn't know what to say to the woman.

"Come and have a drink now," the woman offered, "and I'll tell you about the crystal."

"Thanks," Susan said and followed the woman into the snack bar.

9

YOU MUST BE SPECIAL

Susan sat fiddling with her pop bottle in the wet rings on the table. So many questions were going through her head she didn't know where to start. The woman sat quietly.

Susan glanced up through her lashes and saw the woman was watching her. She looked amused.

"My name is Susan Sinclair," she said in an effort to get the woman talking, "and I'm only ten years old."

"Ten." The woman nodded and smiled. "I was sixteen when the crystal chose me."

"Why did you give it to me?" Susan blurted out.

"I didn't, Susan, not exactly." The woman laid her hand on top of Susan's. "Let me tell the story in my own way." She sipped her coffee and then looked at Susan. "It's hard for me, too, you know."

Susan sat back and clamped her lips shut.

The woman laid her empty coffee cup down and finally began. "My name is Miranda Coleman," she said, nodding to Susan, "and I am about seventy-two years old."

Susan was surprised. Seventy-two was ancient to her.

"I owned the crystal for almost sixty years," the woman continued. "It's not exactly true to say I owned it. No one owns it really. Very few of us are chosen to be its Guardian. You are the Guardian now, the crystal will always be with you." The woman had a deep look in her eyes and stared into the corner of the room.

Susan settled in to listen so as not to miss a word.

"To be a Crystal Guardian is a fine adventure and a great responsibility. The crystals are a force on the planet for righting events that have gone wrong. The Guardians are the people who do the righting. We are drawn to places where there is a wrongness and people who have been wronged. We help set things right."

"But I can't help anyone," Susan blurted out. "I'm ten years old, and most of the time, I need help myself."

Mrs. Coleman smiled. "I suppose it does seem like that to you. But, believe me, the crystal can sense the qualities it needs in a person. You must have them. You saw and felt the crystal in the basket where I placed it."

Susan shook her head. "I'm not special," she said. "There must be some mistake. I can't be expected to help people from all over the place. I'm not even brave."

"Ah, but you are, Susan." Mrs. Coleman smiled. "I attended markets every weekend for three months with the crystal in my basket. You were only the fourth person who even saw it there."

"So, if others saw it, why aren't they this"—Susan flapped her hand—"Crystal Guardian?"

Mrs. Coleman chuckled. "They saw it. They didn't hold it." She looked up at the ceiling with a grin on her face. "One chappy tried to grab it." She shook her head.

"What happened?"

"The crystal jumped away from his hand so quickly that the basket was overset, and the crystals and stones went everywhere."

"What did the guy do?"

"He looked at me, astounded. Then rushed off into the crowd." Mrs. Coleman patted Susan's hand on the table. "You must be a lot braver, smarter, and more resourceful than you think."

Susan's heart sank. "But I'm not. Everybody says I'm not." She shook her head and stared at her hands on the pop bottle.

Mrs. Coleman chuckled. "Well, your depths are definitely hidden, but I'm sure the crystal would not be mistaken. You are very young yet. You will be equal to the task, and your confidence will grow as you learn to use your talents. Anyway, what do other people know?"

"How will I know when I'm going to be sucked up to help someone?" Susan wanted to know.

"Ah." The lady smiled. "The crystal will always surprise you, but keep it near you at all times. You will become more attuned to it. Then you will feel when you are needed and have time to prepare."

"Prepare? How?" Susan could see more problems.

"Well, everyone is different." Mrs. Coleman laughed. "The first time I went on a crystal journey, I arrived in my nightdress."

"I arrived on the ship in my pajamas!" Susan laughed with her.

Mrs. Coleman's eyebrows went up. "I'm surprised, Susan. You have been back to the ship already?"

Susan nodded.

"Well, there must be some urgency involved. You will have to be ready. I have some things in my car that will help you understand how it all works."

As Mrs. Coleman gathered up her purse, Susan asked, "How will I know who I'm supposed to be helping?"

"That's easy," said the lady, scooping her change into her purse and putting her coffee cup back on the tray. "It will be the boy you tossed across the deck. You always come into contact with the person very quickly..."

Her voice faded away because Susan was on her feet and very angry. With her hands clenched at her sides, she gritted out between her teeth, "I wouldn't help him. He's a nasty person. He tried to hit me." She waved her arms. "I wouldn't cross the street to help such a miserable person, and you expect me to travel across time and an ocean?" She shook her head. "Forget it." She took a deep breath and then carried on. "He's skinny. He's ragged. He's rude. He pulled my hair. No way!" She was almost yelling now.

Mrs. Coleman looked angry, too. "You silly girl," she shot back. "You have great opportunities for adventure and learning in front of you, and you're complaining because he isn't exactly like you." Her voice was rising as well. "So his clothes aren't clean, and he's skinny. So he's rude. What do you know? I bet you've never missed a meal in your life, or ever been really cold." She picked up her purse. "You'll learn," she said, shaking her finger. "Oh, you'll learn. And I can see it will have to be the hard way." Mrs. Coleman turned on her heel and marched out the door.

Susan was left standing by the table. "I won't cry. I won't cry. I won't cry," she said over and over to herself. *I still don't know how the crystal works*, she thought as she looked round the snack bar.

Everyone was looking at her. She turned to leave, too. Susan put her pop bottle on the tray and walked the tray to the rack. She walked out the door with her head very low.

"I won't cry. I won't cry," she muttered, but quietly she could hear, "It's a rare gift. It's a rare gift."

10

ALONE

It was too soon for her father and mother to be ready to leave, so Susan had time to kill. She sat under a tree on the edge of the grounds. The sound of the wind soughing through the leaves calmed her. She watched the people moving from table to table up and down the rows of stalls. Everyone in the area came to the flea market to exchange what they no longer wanted for what others no longer wanted. Her dad called it "a form of recycling." It was a very social occasion, with neighbors meeting neighbors and stopping to chat.

It all seemed so normal; she had seen it all hundreds of times in her life. *It should be different*, she thought, and then she realized what had changed. *I'm different*, she decided. *Everyone else is still the same.*

Susan couldn't decide; was that good or bad?

I'm stuck with the crystal, she thought and dug it out of her pocket. Could she feel some sort of draw from it? She didn't think so. She still liked it, and it felt comfortable in her hand. She stared into its depth, trying to sense something from it, anything, but nothing came. She felt nothing.

In fact she felt quite numb. She knew now the crystal was going to pull her into adventures whether she liked it or not. Mrs. Coleman had made her understand. *I wish I hadn't sounded off about the nasty boy,* she thought. *Then Mrs. Coleman wouldn't be so angry with me.* Susan felt like kicking herself. She had annoyed the one person who could help her.

I'm all alone now, she thought and got to her feet. She couldn't sit still another minute. She hurried toward the van, hoping her parents would finish early.

While she walked, she searched the crowds for her parents, but her inner eye was seeing the crowd of people on the ship. They were so different, poor, ragged, cold, and hungry. She thought of the nasty boy, too.

I don't even know his name, she realized. *Maybe he's all alone. I can't keep calling him the nasty boy.* Try as she might, she couldn't remember seeing him with anyone else. *Except for that first time when he was being chased by the bigger boy and he slipped and fell at my feet.* Susan smiled at the memory.

Then she saw her family. Her father, picking through a box of old books. Her mother, chatting with a woman over one of her carvings. Susan ran forward with a surge of relief and was happy just to stand beside her mother and let the conversation wash over her.

There, next to the comfort of her parents, Susan's mind wandered to how different life was on the ship. *Maybe I can help*, she thought. *At least I'll try*. Her hand stroked the denim of her jeans, the pocket where the crystal nestled. She felt at peace inside. She was sure she had made the right decision.

11

STORMY WEATHER

All that day, Susan gathered things she thought would be useful for the boy on the ship. She sneaked an old coat from the rack in the mudroom. She stuffed granola bars in the pockets, along with an apple and an orange. Susan remembered learning in history class about scurvy and how people on sailing ships ate oranges and lemons to keep it away.

That night, after her mother had turned out the light, Susan climbed back into her jeans and a warm sweater. She pulled the big woolly coat over her other clothes, and clasping the little knife in one hand and her crystal in the other, she lay down to sleep.

She had a list in her head, and she ran over and over it in the darkness.

Give him back his knife.
Find out his name.
Give him the coat.
Give him back his knife…
Find out…

Finally, on about the fifth run-through, Susan slept.

■ ■ ■

"I tol' ye afore, laddie." Someone was shaking Susan madly. "Ye can't be sleepin' in the gangway. Now ge' along." The same sailor shoved her roughly out onto the deck to stumble against the boxes and bundles again.

Night. The wind howled in the rigging, and before she'd stepped two paces, the deck heaved up and hit her. *Bang.* Down she went, splayed out. Icy ocean water washed down the deck. The ship shuddered up the next wave, and the water rushed by and out the scuppers. *Bang.* Down again. Susan skidded, wet and shocked, across the deck and into a pile of boxes.

At least the wind was a little quieter here, but the ship heaved and tossed like a wild horse, trying to escape the storm. Hunched up as small as she could be, Susan opened one eye and stared straight at the nasty boy. They were pitched together into a corner.

She was cold, but his lips were blue.

Lightning flashed, and in its glare, she could see his face plainly—teeth chattering, eyes squeezed shut, the boy was totally turned in on himself. Even when the darkness returned, Susan could see him. He looked awful. He had no coat. He looked so small and helpless. Susan crawled over and pulled him inside the big coat.

Even though the wool on the outside was wet, the inside was still dry and warm. She rubbed the boy's hands; they were icy. *I hope he's not dead,* she worried as she rubbed. She didn't know what else to do. Wanting to help someone wasn't the same as actually helping.

All night through the horrible storm, she lay there, holding the boy against her. She didn't think he was dead. *Maybe it's just the movement of the ship making him move,* she fretted.

The storm went on and on; the ship wallowed and gurgled. It would throw its bow up to climb a wave and then slide under as the ship crashed down. All the sails were furled. Just one small one at the front was left up, and it was slapping and flapping most of the time as the ship wallowed on.

I hope someone knows where we're going, Susan thought as she braced herself against the crash of another wave. She wasn't sure which were the worst, the waves the ship climbed over or the ones the ship crashed through. She had no idea why the ship hadn't smashed to pieces.

■ ■ ■

When Susan woke, the sea was calm again, and the ship slapped smoothly over the waves. All was quiet. The hissing of the ship through the ocean and the drip of water draining out of the sails were the only sounds she heard.

How could I ever sleep she wondered, trying to move. The boy woke with a start. He pushed and leaped. Susan tumbled in a heap, and the boy was out on the deck. Hands out, legs wide apart, he glared at her.

"What do you think you're doing?" he growled.

Now don't blow it, Susan, she thought as she climbed slowly and stiffly to her feet. *You want to help this kid.*

She gestured to the coat, which was still hanging on her shoulders. "I shared my coat with you during the storm."

"Who asked you?" The boy jutted his chin out belligerently.

Susan clamped her mouth shut. She just didn't know how to talk to someone who was always so unfriendly.

"I suppose you expect me to thank you now," said the boy, and with a toss of his head, he turned on his heel and went to strut off up the deck. He must have turned too sharply, though, because instead of strutting, he sat down, *plomp* on the deck. He looked so surprised.

Susan laughed. She couldn't help it. It was all too much. The storm, her fear, the crystal, her whole life was upside down—just like the boy. She couldn't stop. She crowed. She held her sides. She dropped to the deck. There were tears on her cheeks, it was so funny.

Out of the corner of her eye, Susan noticed the boy wasn't moving. He'd sat down, fallen on his back, and not moved again.

"Oh no." Susan scrambled over the deck to where he lay. He was very still. She rubbed his wrists, but he didn't stir. How thin he looked.

Susan grabbed his bony wrist and pulled him back into the shelter of the boxes.

"Leave me alone," he mumbled, trying to struggle.

Taking off the coat, she carefully rolled him inside it. He was too weak to stop her, and even though he struggled, she soon had him bundled up and propped against the boxes. Then she remembered the food in the pockets. She pulled out the little store and tried to decide what would be best for him. The orange seemed like a good idea. She peeled it quickly and pulled off a segment. She held it to his mouth.

The fresh, tangy smell of the orange was wonderful against the salt, tarry stench of the ship. Once the boy had smelled it, he gobbled the segment greedily.

"Take your time, not too fast." Susan remembered something about how very hungry people shouldn't eat too much too fast. She'd seen it on television.

She slowly pulled off another segment of the orange. The boy's eyes never left her hands.

"My name's Susan. What's yours?" She held up the segment.

"Jeremy Faraday." He darted his head forward and gulped the orange from her hand.

"Please, eat more slowly. You'll make yourself sick." Susan pulled off another segment. "Why are you so hungry?"

The boy didn't answer, but he chewed this segment before swallowing it. Susan looked up, and his green eyes were looking straight into her blue ones.

"I've come to help you," she tried to explain. "You are cold and hungry and on this awful ship, and I don't quite understand why, but I'm supposed to help you. I don't even know how to help you."

Jeremy was still staring right into her eyes. He opened his mouth. She put in some orange. He chewed slowly and swallowed. His eyes never left hers.

He ate three more segments as Susan fed him slowly. It was as if they were locked in time. Then, with Susan watching, his eyes softened, and his whole face took on a more open look. Susan knew a decision had been made.

Then a tear trickled out of the corner of Jeremy's eye. His hands were muffled in the coat, so the tear tracked a course down his cheek. Susan hadn't wanted to make him cry. She leaned forward and wiped the tear away with her finger. How had she ever thought Jeremy was nasty?

"Where are your parents?"

"Dead."

"How?"

And the whole awful story came tumbling out, while Susan quietly fed Jeremy the rest of the orange and most of a granola bar.

Jeremy grew up in a small village in England with his parents and his younger sister, Katie. They were poor but lived well enough. His father got occasional work in the fields for the local lord, and they had two sheep and a cow that grazed on the common. His mother spun the wool from the sheep into thread and wove it into cloth that she could then sell.

But the lord fenced in the common. Then there was nowhere for the sheep or the cow to graze, and so they had to sell them. Everyone in the village was trying to sell their beasts because they could no longer graze them. There were no buyers, so they got very little money for the sheep and even less for the cow.

They traveled to the city, and Jeremy's father and mother began work in one of the new factories that had opened up. His mother was spinning and weaving again, but now she worked on a huge machine. The air was dirty. The machine was loud and dangerous. They could barely live on the money they earned.

His parents heard about America. It was better there. They decided it was time to leave England and travel to the New World. The passage to New York for themselves, Jeremy, and his sister, Katie, had taken every coin they possessed, and even then they could only afford to travel in steerage.

This was the cheapest way to travel on the ship. All the steerage families were herded together in an area below decks. Each family was allotted an area about the size of a double bed in which to stow all their possessions and themselves. The allotments were stacked three high like bunks.

Single men and single women had separate places on the ship, but it was no better for them.

The food was poor and not plentiful, but there was the promise of a new and rich land in America. There, fortunes could be made, so people made the journey.

Susan was astounded; Jeremy's life was so different from her own.

"But, Jeremy, why are you out on the deck in the cold?"

Within days of leaving Plymouth, Katie fell ill with a fever. As she became sicker and sicker, Jeremy's mother became worn down with caring for her. Even below decks, in steerage, it was cold and crowded. Clothing and blankets would not dry. There was no proper place to wash yourself or your clothes. There were only two lots of toilets for the hundreds of passengers in steerage. Even before Katie died, her mother was shivering and shaking, burning hot one moment and deathly cold the next.

Jeremy watched his mother die, too, and then his father just gave up. He sat. He wouldn't eat or seek shelter. Within two weeks of starting the voyage, his father died, too. His dead body was slipped over the side into the deep. Jeremy was all alone, small, frightened, and unable to defend himself from the casual brutality of the other steerage passengers.

The few possessions the family had were taken from him piece by piece. The other families even took over the space in steerage his family had occupied. Jeremy tried to move into the men-only area, but Slade and his cronies pushed him out of there.

His father's knife was all he still had from his family. And Susan had casually taken it away from him. Then Jeremy had nothing.

"I can help you." Susan reached out her hand to Jeremy. "I'm sorry I was mean to you. I didn't understand what it was like."

Jeremy looked at her sideways. "Why wouldn't you?" he said slowly. "You must be on the ship somewhere." He sat up straighter, as though he'd just had a thought. "If you've got a cabin to sleep in, what are you doing on the deck?"

Susan opened her mouth, but no answer came. She wasn't completely sure what was happening herself. She didn't want to try to explain her life to a poor, starving boy on a heaving sailing ship, over a hundred years in her past.

But Jeremy had had another thought.

"Susan," he said. "That's a funny name for a boy." He moved forward to look more closely at her.

Uh-oh. Susan did not want to explain.

"I have to go," she said, scrambling to her feet. "I'll come again and bring more food for you." Her hand sneaked into her pocket and clutched the crystal.

Nothing happened. She was still firmly standing on the wooden deck.

"Your knife is in that pocket," she said, pointing to the coat Jeremy was now wearing. She clutched the crystal tighter. *Come on. Come on, crystal,* she thought desperately. *Let's go.*

Jeremy was standing up, too. He was plainly puzzled, but he thrust his hand in the pocket and brought out the knife. A look of relief spread across his face.

Oh, I wish I was home in bed, thought Susan. *Let's go, crystal. Now!* And the sliding, slipping, pulling came, and she lurched off the deck and landed in her bed. It felt good.

12

HOME AGAIN

"Susan, get up. I've called you three times already." Susan's mother tapped her shoulder.

Susan groaned. She rolled over onto her back and turned bleary eyes on her mother. "What time is it?"

"Almost half past nine. Get up. I have an appointment in town, and I'll be late." From the door, her mother turned. "I'm going down to put your toast in. Hurry!"

Susan groaned again. She could smell the salt tang of the sea, and it felt like the bed was rocking under her. She had just arrived back. She had been awake most of the night in the storm. She had had a long talk with Jeremy. Now she had to get up and go to town with her mother. How was she going to get through the day?

Susan groaned as she tumbled out of bed. She was fully clothed and stank of salt, sea, tar, and other things she didn't want to think about. She bundled her clothes into the laundry hamper.

The shower helped—getting out was the hard part. By the time she had dressed and brushed her hair, she felt awake at least. Susan yawned again. She dragged herself down the stairs for breakfast.

"You look terrible, Suzie Blue Moon." Dad brushed her hair back as she sat over her toast.

"Are you ill?" Mum glanced at her from the sink.

Susan didn't know what to say. She didn't want to lie.

"I...I didn't sleep very well. I'm not sick. I'm just tired."

Dad reached over and ruffled her hair. "You look like you spent all night in a storm."

Susan looked up quickly. Did they know?

"You need to go back to bed," her father continued. "No sense pushing it."

Her mother dried her hands and went to the phone. "I'll change my appointment to this afternoon."

■ ■ ■

After breakfast Susan went straight back to bed. The cool, clean sheets and the soft mattress felt wonderful. She wriggled to make a cocoon, and the duvet settled around her like her mother's arms. She felt these things as if for the first time. It had never occurred to her before that some people, in other times, didn't have all she had. She hoped Jeremy was all right. With these thoughts, she slipped into sleep.

■ ■ ■

A bird sitting on the windowsill, singing its heart out, woke Susan around lunchtime. She stretched slowly in the warm covers and just reveled in the sound.

As her senses returned her from sleep, she noticed the funny smell. Her clothes in the hamper stank. *I better get those washed before Mum notices,* she thought. She dressed quickly, and holding the clothes as far away from her nose as she could, she headed downstairs to the laundry room.

Her mother worked in her studio whenever she could, so Susan had the house to herself for a little while. She shoveled in extra soap and set the wash cycle to heavy-duty.

She found cheese, ham, and a tomato in the fridge, and made herself a sandwich. Susan sat at the spotless kitchen table, and her delicious, fresh sandwich rested on a pretty china plate. She also had a glass full to the brim with orange juice. It was all different. No, she corrected herself, s*he* was different. The house, the kitchen, were the same. But now when she looked at the things that had always surrounded her, she thought of Jeremy and what his life was like. It made the whole kitchen seem more precious. She ate her sandwich slowly, savoring every bite.

Sleeping is going to be a problem. I can't take a day off every time I go to help Jeremy. What happens when the summer holidays are over? Mum and Dad will be packing me off to the doctor if I'm tired all the time. I need more food for Jeremy. At least he's warm now, in Dad's old coat. Her mind ran on, planning and scheming what she could do next and what would be the best things to take to Jeremy.

As she lifted the laundry out of the machine and into the dryer, she remembered Mrs. Coleman saying, "It's a rare gift." Now she could agree. It was. The crystal had certainly led her into adventures. And she really had helped Jeremy. She had never been able to help anyone before.

I like knowing I helped. I hated the storm, though. Scary. Susan shut the dryer door. *I kinda like Jeremy, even though he was really horrible to start.*

As she pushed the button to start the drying cycle, she had another thought. *I guess he was really angry and scared to start. So much horrible stuff happened to him.*

Susan swallowed. She remembered being angry with Mrs. Coleman. *Scared. Me too. I should say I'm sorry,* she thought. *I wonder if I can phone her.* Susan headed straight for the phone.

She wanted to do this before all her old doubts and maybes came flooding in like usual. She turned to the Cs, moving quickly before she could think of a million reasons why she shouldn't call "Miranda Coleman, Guardian of the crystal"—former Guardian of the crystal. Susan patted her pocket.

The number was there, right in the directory, right in town. She punched in the numbers. She heard the phone ringing.

"Hello, this is Miranda Coleman. I'm not here right now. Leave your number if you like."

Susan hung up in disappointment. Such an ordinary message from someone who had owned a crystal that dragged her off to all kinds of wonderful adventures. She hoped she would be able to pluck up the nerve to call again. She wrote a note to herself. Phone Miranda Coleman. Notes helped her remember. She put it on her dresser when she went upstairs to spread out her duvet.

13

AT THE LIBRARY

"Susan, you did your washing." Mum sounded pleased. Susan folded the last piece and put it on top of the pile. Her mum padded in from the mudroom in her socks. Susan looked. Her mum. Here with her. Alive. Susan gulped.

Mrs. Sinclair reached back and pulled the elastic from her ponytail. She shook her head, and her dark, straight hair fell around her shoulders. She liked to keep it back off her face while she carved. She rolled down the sleeves of the tie-dyed tunic she wore over her jeans. She gave Susan a hug. "Do you feel rested now?"

"Oh sure, Mum, I had a great sleep." Susan picked up the bundle of clean clothes and followed her mum into the kitchen.

"Put them upstairs, then," said her mum. "If you're really all right, I have an appointment at the spa, so you can come with me."

Big groan. Boring. She had sat through a couple of hours while Mum "had the works" before. Susan sighed.

■ ■ ■

Ten minutes in the spa and Susan was bored. The magazines were full of skinny women in fabulous clothes or gorgeous houses nobody could possibly be comfortable in. Susan wandered outside to look up and down the street.

The library. The library was good. She told her mum where she would be, then wandered down the street and into the cool, quiet building.

Susan didn't know the town library well. She had visited only a couple of times with her class. Susan wandered aimlessly through the shelves.

A large book on the bottom shelf attracted her attention. Instead of standing up straight, it lay face up on the shelf. The front cover showed a picture of a large wooden sailing ship. It looked similar to Jeremy's ship. She picked it up carefully and tiptoed along the row, looking for a table.

The table she found was huge. A man sat at one end, and so she moved to put her book down at the other. But Susan misjudged the height of the table, and the book dropped with a loud thud. The sound echoed off the stacks and magnified, until the whole library seemed to be booming, "*Susan dropped a bo-ok.*" The man glared down the table at her.

"You broke my concentration," he scowled. "Sit elsewhere and be quiet." He made shooing gestures with his hands as though Susan were a pet. Susan tiptoed away. She headed for the farthest corner, to get as far as possible from everyone.

Someone was in the corner before her.

A young woman bent over a table, stretching toward a book that had fallen in the corner. The table top was covered. There were books and tins. There was a coiled rope and a couple of rusty hooks. In the middle there was a large glass case. The woman must have heard Susan approach, because she turned around immediately.

"Oh, hey, just what I need." Margaret smiled. Susan knew the woman's name was Margaret because she wore a handwritten library badge pinned to her blouse.

"Can you help me?" Margaret continued. "The book in the corner fell over, and I can't reach it."

Susan liked her instantly.

"I can't reach it, either." she said.

"Ah," agreed Margaret, "but you're small enough to climb up on the table and pick your way through the display to stand the book up." Margaret wriggled her fingers to mimic someone tiptoeing along.

"All right." Susan kicked off her shoes and climbed onto the table. At least Margaret was friendly. This would mean she had helped two people in two days. She began picking her way through the items arranged on the table.

"Whatever you do, don't fall on the glass case," Margaret offered.

With one leg poised for the next delicate step, Susan glanced at the case and then nearly did fall over. She put her toe down quickly and centered herself as she had been taught.

The glass case held a large model of a wooden sailing ship. The ship was in full sail, and tiny boxes and bundles cluttered the deck. Tiny carved wooden figures stood or worked among the bundles. She caught herself peering closer, looking for Jeremy on the deck.

Margaret noticed Susan's scrutiny.

"It's a wonderful model, isn't it?" she said.

Susan had to agree. It brought back all the sights and sensations she had experienced just last night on a real ship with Jeremy.

Centering all her concentration, Susan resolutely turned away from the ship and picked her way through to the fallen book. Standing it up, she noticed it was very similar to the book she had found earlier.

As Susan picked her way back to the table edge, Margaret explained, "I'm going to be a librarian. I'm at the college now, and this is my practicum." Margaret grabbed Susan's hand and steadied her as she climbed off the table. "One of the requirements of my studies is to set up a display, but the only space available was this back corner."

The two stood admiring the table. "The model sailing ship came from the local museum. Most of the artifacts on the table came from there, too," Margaret continued.

"I've been pulling all the sailing ship books I can find." Margaret waved her hand toward the shelves. "I want the display to be a big success. Sailing ships used to come into Nanaimo Harbor, you know."

Susan smiled. "I know where there's another sailing ship book for you." She tiptoed back to the table where she had left the noisy book.

"Thanks, Susan." Margaret was thrilled. "I've been looking for this one. It was listed in the catalog, but must have been wrongly shelved."

Susan climbed back onto the table and set the new book up in the opposite corner of the display. It made the exhibit look more balanced.

In stepping back to admire her handiwork, though, Susan accidentally kicked a tin. Off the table it rattled. The empty tin made a terrible noise when it hit the floor. It rolled under another table, clanking all the way. Susan blushed. She scrambled down from the table and scurried after the tin.

Susan came up, red and breathless, tin in hand.

"I'm so sorry," she whispered. "I'm sorry about the noise." Susan held the tin out to Margaret. "It was clumsy of me to knock the tin."

She looked from the tin to Margaret's face. She was red, too. She looked angry. *Oh no,* thought Susan, *just when I was getting the hang of helping, too.*

Then Margaret exploded. She laughed and laughed. Susan couldn't believe it. Laughing? Then in relief she began to laugh, too. The two of them stood there in the back corner of the library, both clutching the noisy tin and trying to laugh quietly. Eventually they sat on the floor, leaning against each other, with the occasional giggle still trickling out of one of them or the other.

Susan leaned over close to Margaret and whispered, "Shouldn't we be quiet?"

Margaret shook her head. "It's a library, not a tomb." She got to her feet. "You're expected to respect other people's space, but you don't have to apologize for laughing."

Susan climbed to her feet, too. "I'll put the tin back." She felt better about the library. As though she belonged.

In stretching out her hand with the tin, Susan noticed detail on it for the first time. "Groves Finest Teas," it said. The next line read, "Rajah Blend." The tin showed a picture of a rajah—Susan assumed it was a rajah. He wore a huge turban, and was sitting on a big cushion on a throne. A servant, also wearing a turban and very fancy clothes, was serving him tea. In the background of the picture, there were other servants shown. One held a feather fan and was obviously keeping the rajah cool. A magnificent tiger curled at the rajah's feet. It stared straight out of the picture and looked very fierce.

Susan pushed the tin gently to get it in exactly the right spot again. Oops, she noticed a dent in the side. "I hope I didn't do that when I knocked it off the table."

"No," Margaret assured her. "It was already dented."

"Why would a museum keep a beat-up old tin?" Susan mused. "Why would you put it in your display about sailing ships?"

"Ah." Margaret picked up the tin and rubbed it in her hands. "See, the tin was for tea."

Susan rubbed the tiger's face with her finger.

"In olden times, tea was very valuable," Margaret continued.

Susan looked up in surprise. Her mother had bags and bags of tea in the cupboard, and Susan thought it was inexpensive to buy.

Margaret saw her question.

"Tea used to be very rare," she went on. "It was only grown in China for the longest time, and then they found it in India as well. Every year the sailing ships loaded up with tea at the end of the growing season and raced back to home port. The first crew back made their fortune. They charged whatever they wanted for their cargo."

Susan could imagine people rushing down to the harbor when the sails were sighted. Or did they have to wait in line at a store to buy the tea?

"Lots of improvements were made to sailing ships," Margaret continued, "to make them sail faster to win the race. They called the ships clippers. So tea was actually very important to sailing ships. And that's why—"

"You have the tea tin in your sailing ship display." Susan finished the sentence with a grin.

"That's right," Margaret agreed, slipping the tin back into place.

■ ■ ■

"There you are, Susan." Her mother came through the bookcases. "I've been looking everywhere for you."

"Sorry." Susan swung her foot. "I was helping Margaret with the display."

"I see." Susan's mum came closer. "It looks very interesting."

"Look at the picture on the tin, Mum." Susan pulled her mother closer to the display.

"You know, we have a tea tin at home. It was your grandfather's," Susan's mother said.

Margaret had heard, and her eyes brightened. "Could I borrow it for my display? It would be great to have another one."

"Sure. I'll dig it out of the cupboard and clean it up when I get home. Susan, you remind me so I don't forget."

As they were leaving, Susan looked back at the display. It looked interesting back there in the corner.

14

ANOTHER ARGUMENT

Soon after they arrived home, the phone rang, and it was Judy.

"Sue Sue, you didn't answer the phone this morning. Are you OK? I was worried about you. I'm coming right over to see you right now. You stay right there." And Judy hung up.

Susan hung up, too.

"Was that a wrong number?" asked her mother, coming in from hanging up her jacket.

Susan shook her head. "No, it was Judy."

"You didn't say a word."

Susan shrugged and smiled. "It was Judy. She's coming over."

Susan went out to wait by the gate. She had lived some real adventures since their conversation about the crystals. As she walked along the driveway, she tried to decide whether to tell Judy what had happened. Would Judy believe her? It all seemed very fantastic.

Judy's my friend, she thought with a smile. *She trusts me. If I say it's true, she'll believe me. How excited Judy will be?* She leaned over the gate and waved as Judy came coasting down the little hill.

Susan was ready to launch straight into her tale as Judy reached the gate, but Judy was talking even before she stopped pedaling.

"Sue Sue, where were you?" she wanted to know.

"I was too tired." Susan held the gate open, and Judy pushed her bike through. "I was too tired, because I was awake all night."

And Susan launched into her story. As she began to tell it, she realized it sounded more exciting and adventurous in the telling than it had in the living. Very soon she was talking nineteen to the dozen. Judy pushed her bike alongside as the two walked up the drive to the front porch. She said not a word. She just looked at Susan sideways as Susan kept talking and talking. All about crystals and sailing ships and the library and tea and Jeremy. Susan went on and on. She was enjoying telling the story. *It's great to share the adventure with Judy,* she thought.

They were sitting on the porch steps by the time Susan finished, and then she had a brilliant idea. She turned to Judy and tugged her sleeve.

"Judy, why don't you come tonight and sleep over? Then maybe the crystal will pull you along, too, and we can share the adventure."

"Why would I want to have a sleepover with such a liar?" Judy sprang up and pulled her sleeve out of Susan's hands. She was red in the face, and her eyes blazed. Hands on hips, she turned and scowled down at Susan sitting on the steps.

"Susan Sinclair, you are so stupid to think I would believe such a stupid story. I know you have a good imagination, but where did you get such fibs?" She jerked on the handlebars of her bike. "I'm not staying around here to listen to such talk." She set her foot on the pedal. "Just because you have a new crystal is no need to make up stories about it." She yelled back over her shoulder, "My crystal is wonderful, and it keeps me healthy." Then she stood on the pedals and rode up the driveway as quickly as she could.

Susan sat alone with her mouth open. *I guess the story is hard to believe*, she thought. *I barely believe it myself.*

Now the crystal had cost her a friend. She pulled it from her pocket and opened the brown velvet bag. The crystal lay quiet in her hand. She held it up to the light. It sparkled in the sun, just like an ordinary crystal. She knew it wasn't, though—ordinary, that is.

What did she believe? She used the point of the crystal to draw squiggles in the dust at her feet. She owned a crystal—or maybe the crystal owned her. It sucked her into the past, onto the deck of a sailing ship. Susan sighed. She drew a sailing ship in the dust. Then quickly she brushed all the scratching away with her foot and looked up, smiling.

It doesn't matter what I believe, she realized. *I was on the ship; I smelled of tar and salt. I touched Jeremy; I felt him shiver. He ate the orange; my hands were sticky. It is happening. I just have to do what I can to help.*

"So crystal," she said, peering into its depths, "what's next?"

15

THE VALUE OF TEA

After supper, while her mother and father were drinking their coffee, Susan remembered the tea.

Tea. Margaret said that tea cost a lot more in Jeremy's time. I wonder....

Susan folded and refolded her napkin. *Maybe? Maybe I could get tea here and take it back to him. Would that work?*

"How much does tea cost?" she blurted out.

"Not very much," her mother replied. "I get a hundred tea bags for a couple of dollars."

Susan was surprised and excited at the same time. She could buy enough tea bags with her allowance to make Jeremy rich. Then she wouldn't have to keep taking him food every night for the rest of her life.

■ ■ ■

Before tumbling into bed that night, she tiptoed back to the kitchen. She loaded up her pockets with apples and cookies. Then she added a handful of tea bags to her hoard and went quietly up to her room. *Maybe he can trade them for a warm place to sleep,* she thought.

She went to sleep clutching the crystal in her hand— and woke on the ship.

It was nighttime and bitterly cold. She zipped up her parka and snapped all the fasteners. She wanted to find Jeremy as quickly as possible and get home to bed. But where was he?

Susan tiptoed across the deck, peering into all the nooks and crannies. The deck heaved gently, and the ship hissed through the water at a good speed. All the sails were up and straining in the wind. There was a faint crackling sound in the air, and when Susan grabbed one of the rigging lines, she discovered the ropes were frozen. The crackling she heard was the ice snapping as the ropes flexed and gave under the movement of the ship. Ice. Susan rubbed her hands together, they ached. It was so cold her fingers felt stiff.

Susan worked her way around the deck, looking in every hiding place she could think of. Nowhere could she find Jeremy.

At last she reached the very stern. She crouched on the sheltered side of a coil of rope. Susan blew some warmth back into her hands while she tried to think. The wind was whistling in the rigging, making an eerie sound. The slap and crackle of the ropes joined with the groan and creak of the ship's timbers as it sailed on toward America.

Then Susan noticed another sound, low and intermittent. She had never heard such a sound before, but got up to investigate. She found Jeremy, huddled into a tight ball, hands clasped over his head.

"Jeremy, are you all right?" Susan hurried over and put her hand on his shoulder. He started up, hands out, ready to defend himself. He looked terrible. The coat was gone, and his face was bruised and cut. His right eye was swollen shut.

"Jeremy, what happened?"

Jeremy slumped to the deck. "Oh, Susan, I lost the coat. I fought, I really did. But he was stronger than me, and he just took it."

Susan pulled off her parka and snuggled Jeremy up tight against the coil of rope and put her parka over the two of them.

"Don't worry about the coat. I'll get you another one."

She could already see the one she would bring. It was in the mudroom. Her uncle John left it when he went to Australia years ago. He didn't need it.

"Here," she said, handing him an apple from her pockets.

But Jeremy didn't reach out for the food; he just looked at her and didn't move.

"Here, eat this," she said.

Still he didn't move.

"Jeremy, what is it?"

"How can you get me another coat? How can you bring me an apple? Even the first-class passengers don't have fresh apples. Where do you go when you disappear? How can this coat be so warm when it doesn't even feel woolly?" Then he grabbed the apple in both hands and took a huge bite. He rolled his eyes as he chewed quickly.

He sounds like Judy, Susan thought with a pang.

Jeremy swallowed. "And another thing. I've never heard of a boy called Susan."

Susan swallowed. *How much should I explain,* she wondered. *Judy didn't believe me, and she was my best friend. I don't want Jeremy yelling at me again.* She shook her head. *What if he calls me a liar like Judy did?* She didn't know what to do. To stall for time, she reached into her pocket to get one of the cookies.

Her hand closed around the crystal instead, and she drew it out. When she noticed she was holding the crystal, she quickly tried to thrust it back into her pocket, but Jeremy had seen. He grabbed her hand.

"What's that?" he wanted to know.

Susan opened her hand. "It's my crystal," she said. She held it up high so Jeremy could see it better. It twinkled in the starlight.

Jeremy stared at it. Not touching it, just staring.

"You must be very rich," was all he said in the end.

"No, no, we're not rich." Susan wanted to assure him. "We live in the country, my mother carves stone, and my father writes articles for magazines. We're just ordinary."

"You don't sound ordinary, and you don't speak ordinary. You're not ordinary. You feed me better food than anyone else on the ship has. How do you do that?"

Then Jeremy just stared at her.

Susan dropped her eyes to her crystal. *Mother. Father.* A great welling of longing and fear swept over Susan. *They are so far away.*

When Susan looked up again Jeremy still sat staring.

I need to tell somebody. I need someone else to know what is happening to me. Maybe I will be able to make more sense out of what's happening if I tell Jeremy.

Susan gulped. *I need a friend.*

And then Susan started her story, and Jeremy listened. Jeremy nodded in the places that he remembered too. He patted Susan's hand when she told him about Judy and the argument they had.

Just then.

Clatter. Bang.

Susan and Jeremy looked up, startled. Slade stood within arm's reach. The coat, that he wore, was caught in the rack of belaying pins.

Before Susan and Jeremy could react, Slade tugged hard on the coat to get it free, and another pin dropped to the deck with a clatter. Susan's hand convulsively closed over the crystal, but it was too late. Slade was on them, flailing right and left. Susan was knocked to the deck. Jeremy tried to strike out at Slade, but was no match for the bigger boy. Susan tried to clamber to her feet, but Slade's hand closed around her wrist like a vise.

"Give me that," he snarled in Susan's ear, as he shook her hand violently. "It's mine now. I'm Slade, and I take whatever I want, and you have no say in it."

Susan kicked out at him, but he was holding her too tightly for her to put any strength into it. Gradually he forced her hand open, and he grabbed greedily at her crystal.

Once he had the crystal safe, Slade threw her roughly away and, cuffing Jeremy hard on the side of the head, strolled off, chuckling quietly. He thrust the crystal deep into the pocket of Susan's father's old coat.

Susan and Jeremy lay, stunned, on the deck. Susan's ears rang from her rough landing. *He's stolen my crystal. What will I do? He's so big. He's stolen it.* Susan drew a shuddering breath. And then came the worst thought of all. *Maybe he's the Guardian of the Crystal now.*

She reached out and pulled her parka over the two of them. At least they still had that. They huddled together for warmth.

16

STRANDED

Susan awoke to the sound of someone sobbing deep, gut wrenching sobs that spoke of great sorrow. Jeremy stirred next to her. As soon as she opened her eyes, it all came flooding back. She was in a lot of trouble. Her parents had probably missed her by now. They would be worried sick.

Susan sat up and looked around. Down the deck, a shabby woman was cradling a child to her chest. Her head was buried in the child's neck, and her shoulders shook with the force of the sobs racking through her body. A crowd had gathered. People stood silently watching.

Sailors marched down the deck, pushing people out of the way. "C'mon now, c'mon now. Give us room," the leader yelled as they came up to the woman. One sailor knelt beside the woman and tried to pull the child from her arms. The woman resisted and began to scream and yell. She looked up at the sailor with pleading in her eyes, but the sailor was stronger and pulled the child away.

"The babe's dead, ma'am," the sailor gruffed. "Died in the night, he did." He held the woman off with one hand. "You have to leave him to us now."

Other women clustered around to comfort the sobbing woman.

Susan stared. She couldn't believe what she was seeing.

Quickly two sailors wrapped the little body in sailcloth, and, with a few deft strokes, sewed the sail shut. There was a board balanced on the rail of the ship, and the little bag containing the body was laid out on the board.

Without any ceremony, the body was dumped into the sea. "God bless ye', child," the sailor said as he clumped up the deck to other duties.

The little bag bobbed on the waves for a moment and then it began to sink. It soon disappeared into the sea.

She turned to look at Jeremy, shivering in the morning cold. *That's what they did to his family.* Susan looked at Jeremy with new eyes. He was huddled in on himself. Tears streaked down his cheeks. *It could have been Jeremy going over the side, wrapped in a sail. He could have frozen to death overnight.* Her eyes opened very wide. *Or even me.* Susan shuddered and rubbed her arms to get warm.

Ow. She was stiff and cold, and hungry and dirty. She chewed her knuckles. *How will I get home,* she worried.

"Good morning." Jeremy was on his feet, too. He stretched his arms and shook his shoulders to get the kinks out. Then he looked at her and smiled crookedly. "I thought you'd have vanished again."

"I'd like to," Susan said, jumping from foot to foot to get warm. "I'd really like to, but..." Susan gulped.

Jeremy nodded, looking abashed. "Oh yes, you need your crystal."

"I'm hungry." She didn't want to think about it. "How do we get food?"

"Right." Jeremy looked at her sideways. "They bring out food just after dawn. If we hurry, we might get some." He grabbed her arm, and together they hurried across the deck.

A large knot of people clustered around one of the masts. As soon as they came up on the back of the crowd, Jeremy lifted his elbows and, using them like oars, ploughed into the people, jostling and pushing.

Susan stopped short. She couldn't do it. But Jeremy was thrusting through. Occasionally someone cuffed his head or pushed him out of the way, but he was gradually disappearing into the press of bodies.

I'll wait, Susan thought and sat on a coiled rope. She thrust her hands into her pockets to keep them warm and watched the crowd.

She recognized her father's old coat before she recognized the boy inside it as Slade. He was seated on a box with his hands full of food. He was laughing with some other tough-looking characters who were sprawled around him. Susan crouched down out of sight. Everything seemed so impossible.

"Oh, Mum, I'm all right really. I'll get home again somehow," Susan whispered.

Jeremy touched her on the sleeve. "I got as much as I could," he said, holding out a dry biscuit. "There's not much left at this time of the voyage."

"When will you arrive?" Susan asked.

"The sailors say we should sight land today and then be in New York tonight—if the weather holds and the wind keeps blowing from this quarter."

Susan took a biscuit and began to nibble at a corner.

"We have to hide." Jeremy pulled her along. "If we stay out here, Slade might take our biscuits."

The two sneaked off along the deck to find a hiding place.

When Susan next lifted her biscuit to her mouth, she noticed movement. On the biscuit. Closer examination showed she was right. "Yuck. This biscuit's got bugs in it."

Jeremy nodded. "Of course, they're weevils."

He took a big bite and munched happily. "This is good. A sailor told me that sometimes the salt water gets into the biscuits, so they're all moldy and soggy. Then there are even more weevils in them. We've been lucky this voyage." He chewed on.

"Take mine." Susan handed him her biscuit and began fishing for crumbs in the pocket of her parka. All gone.

Jeremy was looking at her again; it was time to finish her story. So she took a deep breath and plunged in.

The whole time she spoke, Jeremy said nothing. He looked at her and chewed slowly, but never spoke. So Susan went on and on. It all came out, about the crystal and Judy not speaking to her – she told that bit again. *It's really bugging me that Judy wouldn't listen,* she realized. She told about sneaking the fruit from the cupboards at home. She didn't want to talk about how different her life was.

Finished, she sat waiting for Jeremy to start yelling at her, but he still didn't speak. He was looking at her as though he expected more.

"Oh," Susan remembered, "I'm really a girl, not a boy. We all wear clothes like this in my time, and lots of girls cut their hair short."

Jeremy let out a sigh, as though he had been holding his breath for a long time. "Now I know it's true," he said and put his arm around her shoulders.

"Don't tell anyone else," Susan hurried on. Then she stopped. "Why did you decide my story was true?" Susan laughed a little. "Even I have trouble believing it."

"Ah, it was because you told me you're a girl."

"What difference did that make?"

"Well"—Jeremy leaned back into the coil of rope, looking pleased with himself—"I worked it out. After the first time you brought me food, I looked for you everywhere. I thought you were a cabin passenger, and so I searched all the faces, but you weren't among them. Then I got to thinking about how different your clothes were. For a start I just thought they were rich people's clothes, but no, yours were really different."

"But, Jeremy, you thought I was a boy before."

"Uh-huh," Jeremy agreed, "but every time I thought of you, I thought of my sister. I thought of you the same way I thought of Katie." Jeremy shrugged and grinned. "It seemed pretty silly. But the next time you came, I watched you. As soon as I really looked, I could see you were a girl."

Susan felt a little silly. "Why didn't you say?"

Jeremy shrugged again. "I thought you had your reasons." He stood up and reached down for her hand. "Now I understand what they were. You must have been very surprised and quite frightened when you first appeared."

It was Susan's turn to chuckle. "You can say that again. Believe me, my home is not like this at all."

Home. Susan felt the blood leave her face.

"Jeremy, we have to get my crystal back. My mother and father will be worrying about me by now. It's way past time for me to be out of bed, and they've probably called the police. School starts again soon, and I can't miss that."

"You go to school?"

The question surprised Susan. "Of course, everyone goes to school."

"You can read and write?"

"Yes, everyone can."

Jeremy shuffled his foot and ran his hand along the rail, and then he sighed. "Not here."

"When you land, you will be able to get into a school," Susan said, trying to cheer him up.

"I'll have to work when I get to America."

Susan looked at thin, shivering Jeremy. *He's too young to work,* she thought. *How will he ever find a job? Who will hire such a young boy?*

He saw her looking and squared his shoulders. "I'll have to work so I can live," he said. "America has work for everyone."

That reminded her. Susan reached into her pocket and pulled out the tea bags.

"I brought you these," she said proudly. "They'll help you."

Jeremy leaned forward and peered at the little square paper packets. "What are they?" He poked one gingerly.

"It's tea," Susan explained. "Tea is very valuable in this time."

Jeremy shook his head slowly. "I saw some tea once. It was in the village store. They ordered it for the lord. It was very expensive."

"See, that's what I mean." Susan got excited. "You can sell what I've brought you, and the money will help you get started in America."

Jeremy was still shaking his head. "The tea I saw was little black leaves, all dried up and twisted."

"Oh." Susan felt so silly. Of course tea bags would be a modern invention.

Then she brightened. "The tea's inside."

Quickly she tore open one of the little bags and black dust fell out into Jeremy's hand.

"It still doesn't look like the tea I saw." Jeremy looked disappointed. But he straightened up and smiled at Susan.

"Thank you for thinking of me, and thank you for all your help," he said, taking Susan's hand.

Looking at the tea bags lying in her palm, she shrugged. "Well, it was a thought," she said.

"True." Jeremy squeezed her hand.

She shrugged and threw the bags into the ocean. They both leaned way out to watch the bags floating in the white foam created by the ship's passage.

"Land. Land."

A sailor high up in the rigging pointed happily with his free hand while clinging to the ropes with the other. His bare toes gripped, splayed in the rope, his knees bent to absorb the shudder of the ship as it rose and fell to the swells, he leaned way out, grinning and pointing.

"Land. Land."

Everyone took up the cry. Sailors climbed into the rigging, clinging and laughing, happy the voyage was almost at an end.

Children and adults alike clustered excitedly along the railings, peering out across the billows to the thin blue line barely above the horizon.

17

CAUGHT

The press of people on the railing was far too tight for Jeremy and Susan to push through. Standing on her tip-toes, Susan could see only the ragged backs of the other passengers.

Together, she and Jeremy reached into the rigging and pulled themselves up on the ropes. Soon they were swinging with the ship and could see over the heads of the passengers. Yes, there was land. Misty and blue still, but definitely there to see every time the ship rose on a wave.

"Look, look." A small boy pointed behind them. All heads turned, and people craned to see.

Susan and Jeremy had a good view. Another ship had pulled level with them across the sea. Even though their ship slipped rapidly through the water, even though every sail on its two masts billowed in the wind, this other ship was passing them easily.

"It's a clipper." Susan laughed, remembering her trip to the library and Margaret.

The clipper looked beautiful. She was longer and narrower than their ship. She cut through the water like a knife. Each of her three masts was crammed with sails. Extra ones stretched from the forward mast to the bow. She was traveling so fast and taking so much wind that she heeled over so that the deck was sloped toward them.

An old sailor pulled himself into the rigging beside Jeremy. He wore a scarf tied tightly around his head to keep his hair from blowing in his eyes, but Susan saw a long swatch of hair hanging down his back. It was dipped in tar to keep it back.

Yuck, he looks like a pirate, Susan thought. She asked him if he knew the name of the ship.

"She's the *Flying Cloud*, she is." He leaned out and spat into the sea. "She's a real ship," he added. "Not like this bucket."

"Why don't you sail on one like her then?" Susan asked.

The sailor waved at his legs. "I'd like to, laddie. I'd like to" was all he said.

Following his wave, Susan noticed to her horror that he had a wooden leg. She bit her lip.

Jeremy hadn't noticed, though. "What difference does it make?" he wanted to know.

"The tea trade," the friendly sailor answered. "Tea's where the money is. Ship like her. Beats all the other clippers back to port with the new tea. Everyone makes a fortune."

The sailor pulled on past them, climbing higher to adjust the sails. He used just his arms to pull himself up.

Jeremy watched after the *Flying Cloud*. "Clipper ships and tea," he said quietly.

Susan nodded.

They watched until the clipper ship was a speck of white on the horizon. The passengers finally left the ship's side and began to gather up their belongings for their new life.

Land.

America.

Soon the ship would make port, and everyone could go their own way.

Slade would go his own way, too. Susan's foot slipped in the ropes.

"Jeremy, I have to get the crystal back before the ship docks, or I might lose it completely." She scrambled down to the deck. "I might be stuck here forever."

Jeremy joined her. "I'd look after you, Susan."

"Jeremy, I have to get home. My mum and dad will really miss me. They must be very worried."

"What we need is a plan."

"Do you think the two of us could knock Slade down and grab the crystal?"

"No, I don't." Jeremy shook his head and gently stroked his eye, which still showed bruising from the fight over his coat.

"There are two of us now, and I know some tricks." Susan was getting desperate.

"I remember your tricks," Jeremy said.

Susan looked up quickly. *Not cool, Susan. Reminding him how you threw him across the deck.* But when she caught his eye, he smiled at her.

"But," Jeremy continued, "Slade is always surrounded by his cronies, so we would have to fight three or four, not just one."

The two sighed together.

"Think of another way." Susan tried to think, but no ideas came. All she could think of was how worried her mother would be.

"I know." Jeremy raised his finger. "Every afternoon, Slade snoozes under the tarpaulin over a lifeboat. The others usually go back to their families while he's sleeping, so maybe we can sneak up on him then."

"We better try it."

They both nodded a little.

They went off together to explore the area where Slade usually took his nap. They found a cranny out of the wind where one of them could hide to watch.

"I'll watch first," Susan offered. "You try and get some sleep."

Jeremy was going to protest, but Susan kept talking. "You need your rest so you can be as strong as possible to start your new life. I just need the crystal."

So Susan watched, and Jeremy crept away to find a place to sleep.

It was warm in between the boxes. The wind could not reach her, and the bundle at her back was soft. Susan felt almost comfortable.

She kept her eyes and ears strained for the slightest indication that Slade was about to slip under the tarpaulin.

But the warmth and comfort, together with a sleepless night, had Susan nodding. Her eyes soon drooped, and then she caught her head lolling forward. She lurched awake. This would never do.

Susan couldn't move from her hiding spot, but if she sat much longer, she would be asleep for sure. *I need to concentrate. I have to get the crystal back.*

She didn't want to be stuck in a time where there were bugs in the food. No electricity, no washing machines. Then she thought the very worst: no hot showers and no proper toilets.

Something brushed her leg. She startled up and pulled her leg away. A cat, looked at her, one leg poised to run away. Susan's heart beat so fast she could hear it.

"Hey cat," she whispered as she held out her hand. The cat crept closer and sniffed at her fingers. Susan used her other hand to scratch gently between its ears. The cat came closer.

Susan patted her lap, and the cat sidled up, and curled comfortably there. Susan softly stroked its back. *I'll call you Cat*, she decided.

The cat felt heavy in her lap. *Cat eats well*, she thought. *I wonder who feeds it.*

She fondled its ear. It was all ragged and torn in places. *You've been in fights too, Cat.*

"Oh," she whispered. "You catch the rats." *It's a hard life for everyone on the ship.*

With Cat curled warm in her lap and her hand gently patting its fur, Susan felt a little more relaxed and confident. *I can do this,* she decided. *I will get out of this mess and help Jeremy. We will make it work for us.*

Susan turned her attention outward, listening as hard as she could. *Come on Slade, it's time for your nap.*

She heard two sailors talking close by. They seemed to be whispering, but they were just on the other side of the boxes. Susan strained to hear. She hoped she would be able to understand them.

"Fifteen dollars we'll get, I'm thinking."

"Nah, ten. I reckon," said the second sailor.

"Nay, there are three orphan boys."

"Two. There was only two didn't die. I watched, and I counted."

"Well, you counted wrong."

"Didn't."

"There are three, I be a telling ye. I found another one sleeping on the stairs the other day. Smaller than the other two, though."

"That one. Yeah, that one. Don't know where he came from."

"Yeah, the one with the funny jacket."

Susan gasped. They were talking about her. She was very interested in this conversation.

"And this man will give us five dollars for each of them?"

"Yep, you help me catch 'em, and soon's the ship docks, we hand 'em over and get our money."

"What about immigration and customs and all?"

"Nah, none of that. We sneak them off, see? Nobody knows they're going ashore. We take them quiet like, and we have our papers as sailors to get ashore."

"What does he want with orphan boys?"

The first one laughed.

"What do you care? Just think on spending the money."

"Can we get more for them, think you? Maybe six dollars each."

"Nah, never argue with this guy. Not if you want to make it back to the ship. He says five dollars each, you take five dollars each and tip ya hat and leave quick like."

Susan was awake in every nerve of her body. Here was a new danger.

I have to warn Jeremy, she thought and crept quietly out of her cubby. Cat stretched, and padded along beside her. As they passed the ladder stretching down into the depths of the ship, Cat meowed once, and leaped into the gloom.

Jeremy was curled up in a tight ball, in the sun and out of the wind. Susan touched him gently on the arm.

"Wake up, Jeremy." She shook him harder. "Wake up."

Jeremy sat up quickly. "What's happening?" He looked around. "Is he asleep yet?"

Susan told him about the sailors' conversation.

Jeremy looked glum. What else could go wrong?

He shook his head slowly. "Whatever the sailors are up to doesn't change our other plan. If we can get the crystal, you'll be safe."

"Oh, Jeremy, this is awful. I can't just leave you here to be sold."

"Maybe if you get away, you can find a way to save me later."

"But, Jeremy…" Susan could think of a million objections to the plan. How would she find him? Would the crystal bring her to him or to the ship? What could she do? But Jeremy gave her no time to quibble. He was off along the deck to the hiding place to see if Slade was sleeping in the lifeboat. Susan could only follow close behind.

Two paces in front of her, Jeremy froze. Slade was there and snoozing. One leg dangled over the side of the boat. He was so sure of himself. Susan peered over Jeremy's shoulder.

"Perhaps we should wait until he's sound asleep," she offered.

"Now's the time," Jeremy whispered back. "We can't afford to wait. It may be too late if we do."

Susan hoped her knees wouldn't give way. The two crept closer and closer, placing their feet carefully so as not to make a sound on the heaving deck.

"Try to keep the tarpaulin shading his face," Susan whispered as Jeremy began to lift it.

He nodded slowly and moved his hands ever so carefully under the cloth. Susan did the same.

Trying to make her fingers as light as possible, she began feeling over his clothes for a pocket. "Please let it be in the first pocket I find," she prayed under her breath.

She was lucky; almost immediately she felt a pocket flap under her fingers. Her face was very close to Jeremy's, and by the look in his eyes, he was having some success, too. She carefully lifted the flap and slipped her hand into Slade's pocket.

Slade stirred a little. Susan and Jeremy froze. Slade settled back and was still again. Susan pushed gently into the pocket. A huge, warm hand closed about her wrist. From the way Jeremy was wriggling, she could tell the same had happened to him. They were caught.

18

CAUGHT AGAIN

Slade reared up out of the lifeboat, dangling Susan and Jeremy from his hands. The tarpaulin draped around his shoulders, he stepped out of the boat. As soon as Susan's feet touched the deck she kicked out, but Slade's arms were too long, and he was too strong.

"Well, well, look what Slade's got." He smirked and gave them both a shake.

"Looking for something, were we?" Slade shook them again.

"Should tell the captain I've caught a couple of thieves, I should," he said loudly and thrust the two of them back against the boat. Jeremy staggered against the side. Slade grabbed his shirt front and doubled up his fist for a punch.

Another voice intruded on the scene.

"How lucky for us, Jacky." It was one of the sailors.

"Look, the whole three of 'em—all together, friendly like."

Jackie came up beside his mate. He was the sailor who had shaken Susan awake when she first arrived on the ship.

"Maybe we'll get more for 'em. Them bein' friends an' all, d'y'think, Donno?"

Before Susan could even catch her breath, her wrists were lashed together with rope and the knots tied with a sailor's skill.

"Let me go." She struggled and twisted, but the ropes just seemed to bite more deeply into her skin.

Donno looked up from where he was trussing Jeremy.

"If you don't shut up, Shorty, I'll stuff a gag in y'mouth as well."

Susan believed him. She was quiet.

Jacky was having a bit more trouble with Slade, but these were men, hardened sailors, tough as nails and mean of spirit. Jacky shoved the point of his hook into the side of Slade's nose. Instantly Slade became very still. The hook was just an inch from his eyes. The job was soon done.

The sailors gagged Susan and Jeremy anyway. The cloth through her mouth tasted of sweat and tar. Susan did not want to think what else might be on it. She had to concentrate to breathe.

Donno and Jacky hid the trio in the lifeboat. Susan heard them roping down the tarpaulin. Susan and Jeremy were helpless. They were propped together at the shoulders, with their hands and ankles tied. Slade was bound and gagged and lying across their outstretched legs. He was shivering and looked very scared.

Susan was surprised. *He looks as scared as I feel.*

And there they sat, stiff, sore, and frightened while the ship docked in New York.

19

NEW YORK

When the gangway was lowered, all the passengers hurried off the ship. Susan heard them chatting happily, glad to be away and off to the immigration hall to start their new lives.

Soon most of the sailors had gone ashore as well, bellowing and calling to friends on the dock. They were in a hurry to spend some time ashore before setting off across the Atlantic again.

All Susan could do was listen from the place where she was hidden. Struggling with the ropes tying her hands only made them tighter. Even when Jeremy and she worked together to loosen them, they had no success.

Slade was no help. He just lay there, not moving. Only his eyes seemed alive. Even trussed up, gagged, and scared, he still frightened Susan.

Night fell before Jacky and Donno returned. They whisked back the tarpaulin. They were just dark silhouettes against the twilight of the sky.

Jacky waved his hook in their faces.

"Now, no noise or struggling." He pushed the tip of the hook against Slade's nose again. "Lest you wants to meets me friend here." He waggled the hook back and forth.

They bundled Susan and Jeremy together in a smelly length of sail and hauled them up across Jacky's back. Susan could feel the hook, sharp, through the sail by her ear.

In the smelly dark, Susan heard Slade, though. He was struggling. *Bonk.* All sounds of struggle ceased. And then they were moving—jerked along across Jacky's shoulders. His shoulder dug into her stomach. Susan was almost glad she hadn't eaten.

Thump. Ow. Susan banged into a cart of some sort. The edge dug into her neck.

Thump. Grunt. Jeremy landed next to her. She wriggled around until his elbow moved out of her ribs.

The cart jerked again. *That must be Slade. At least he didn't land on top of us,* Susan thought.

The horrible journey through the streets of New York seemed to go on forever. The wheels of the cart made a grinding sound over the paths they took. The cart bumped a lot, so Susan could tell that the ground was rough. Jacky and Donno were puffing as they pulled the cart along. Susan heard different sounds from time to time, but with no idea of where she was, she could not identify most of them. They were nothing like the sounds of her time anyway. If she could have heard a radio or amplified music or even a bus, she might have had some idea of what was happening outside her blind, bumping, ride. What she heard were sounds from a century past, and most of them were meaningless to her.

Once, she smelled meat cooking. It smelled like chicken. Susan's mouth watered. She was very hungry.

Jacky and Donno were panting and seemed to be staggering on their feet before they finally came to a stop. The cart was tipped, and Susan and Jeremy were dumped into a heap on the ground. Then Slade flopped across her feet. He groaned. The ground was stony under her shoulder.

Susan heard loud knocking. Then she heard a door creak open.

"Good ev'nin', sir." It was Donno talking. "We 'ave some poor horphan boys here for you, like you ask't." Donno's voice sounded all soft and sneaky—not loud and rough like when he talked to them or Jacky—now he was trying to sound educated or posh. But he just sounded oily to Susan.

A stranger answered. "Well, don't just stand there in the light. Bring them in. Bring them in and be quick about it."

Bump. Susan's head banged on the doorstep. It hurt. Donno dragged her across the floor.

A grunt.

Jeremy must have banged his head, too, Susan thought.

The door slammed behind them.

The cloth sail was pulled away, leaving Susan tumbling on the flagstones of an enclosed courtyard. She sat up as quickly as she could, blinking in the sudden light of a candle held very close to her face. The candlelight dazzled her so she couldn't see the person behind the flame. Jeremy banged into her as he was rolled from the sailcloth as well. Slade was next.

Rough hands grabbed her collar and hauled her up. Slade was pushed into her back, and then Jeremy was on his feet, too.

Someone yanked the gags from their mouths.

"Paugh, couldn't you have given them a bath before you brought them here?"

Susan looked up into the face of a tall, elegantly dressed stranger. He wore a red silk dressing gown over his shirt. Snowy white lace frothed at the collar. His shoes had large silver buckles on them. He looked very rich. His face was hard, and his eyes were cold. His nose was wrinkled up. He was waving a lacy handkerchief under it. Susan caught a whiff of rose scent wafting from it. *I suppose I do smell pretty disgusting*, Susan thought and hung her head.

Hard fingers gripped her chin and forced her head up. She tried to keep her head down, but he was too strong for her. He pinched her chin hard. The tall man's candle came very close to her cheek. She felt the heat of it.

"This one looks a bit soft." He pinched her chin harder. Susan bit her lip. She would not cry. She would not.

Jeremy pushed forward to stand shoulder to shoulder with her.

"What's your name, little boy?" the stranger sneered.

"Su—"

"Samuel," Jeremy said quickly, nudging her to be quiet. "He's Samuel, my brother."

The stranger, as quick as a flash, rounded on Jeremy and slapped him hard across the cheek.

"My name's Mr. Brinkley," he snarled. "You can speak when you're spoken to." He brushed his hands on his robe dismissively. "And don't you forget it."

Jeremy glared and rubbed his cheek slowly on his shoulder. Susan moved closer to him. She nudged him gently. *Please don't say any more, Jeremy,* she thought.

Much to Susan's relief, Jeremy was silent. Donno took the opportunity to hold out his hand.

"If the g'nlman would be good enough to pay us now, we'll be on our ways, like," he oiled, leering at Mr. Brinkley.

Jacky nodded behind him, idly polishing his hook along the seam of his pants.

The tall stranger ignored them and turned to a servant who hovered in the doorway across the courtyard. "Pendleton," he snapped.

Pendleton came hurrying over, bobbing and nodding his head as he came.

"Yes, Mr. Brinkley. Yes, sir, Mr. Brinkley."

"Get these 'gentlemen' their ropes," he sneered. "Then get these three below." Mr. Brinkley wrinkled his nose at the three. "Put them in with the others."

"Right away, Mr. Brinkley," Pendleton said, still bobbing and nodding.

With the ropes removed, the servant shoved them in the back to get them moving. Vaguely Susan heard the tall gentleman say, "I'll deal with them in the morning." She stumbled across the courtyard, rubbing her hands to get the circulation moving again.

Pendleton pushed the trio toward a door set in one wall of the courtyard. Susan raised her head to see where she was going and stopped dead in her tracks. Beside the door was a sign. *Welcome, orphan dears,* it said. *Find shelter here with us.* This was a welcome? The words on the sign certainly didn't agree with the treatment they received. Looking up Susan noticed a large banner over the doorway. She squinted to read it in the flickering light. *Rescue Home for Orphan Boys,* the banner said.

"Come on, hurry up." Pendleton shoved her in the back. Away from Mr. Brinkley his demeanor changed. Now he was threatening and swaggering.

Typical bully, Susan thought.

Jeremy and Slade entered the door ahead of Susan. Pendleton pushed her hard. Jeremy caught her when she pitched into him, and that was the only reason Susan didn't fall to her knees.

20

RESCUE HOME FOR ORPHAN BOYS

Pendleton herded them along, but Susan peeped up through her lashes. They stumbled across a large kitchen. It smelled like garbage. Susan coughed to keep the smell away from her nose. The servant drew a key from his pocket and herded them over to another door.

The door creaked open, and in the light of the servant's candle, Susan saw a steep flight of stairs leading down. She peered into the darkness but could not see the bottom.

"Get on with it," Pendleton grunted. "Down you go."

Jeremy grabbed Susan's hand, and together they started hesitantly down the stairs into the dark.

"No, no, I won't go down there." Slade pulled back from Pendleton, who had a firm grip on his arm.

"I'll pay you." Slade began pulling at his pockets. "Set me free. I can pay."

Susan and Jeremy paused on the stairs and turned to watch.

Slade's voice became more confident. He held out a couple of coins. "Here," he said, "let me go. No one will know."

Pendleton laughed harshly and without glancing at the coins, gave Slade a mighty shove in the chest.

With a cry Slade toppled over backward down the stairs. Instinctively Susan and Jeremy gripped each other's hands tighter as Slade banged into them. They slowed his fall. Both of them grabbed the handrails on the sides of the stairs and held on tight.

Slade fell no farther. He caught his balance.

"Lucky you've got friends," Pendleton sneered.

The three looked at one another, a bit surprised, and moved quickly down the stairs together.

The basement was stark stone, damp, and cold.

They eventually came to a halt before a table and chair set against the wall. A line of stout bars partitioned off the end of the basement. As they drew near to this area, Susan could hear rustlings and murmurings in the dark. *Rats.* Susan shuddered.

Pendleton lit a lantern, placed on the table, and in this light Susan could vaguely see a couple of pale faces peering sleepily at them through the bars.

"Now," said Pendleton brusquely, "turn out your pockets and put everything you have on the table."

Jeremy began carefully emptying his pockets. He had very little. A stone from England to place in his new home was all that landed on the table.

Susan schooled her face carefully so as not to show her excitement. She knew Jeremy had a knife and yet somehow he had managed to hide it.

Susan had nothing. Her pockets had been crammed with food before leaving home. It seemed so long ago. Now it was all gone. Her pockets were empty.

The servant shook his head.

"Fine, well-fed boy like you. Put your stuff on the table."

Susan shook her head. "I have nothing," she said.

"Last chance." Pendleton came up close and stood over her. "Do it now."

Susan glared. No one should be treated like this.

"This is a rescue home for orphan boys, not a jail." She placed her hands on her hips. "I have no—" She stopped speaking because Pendleton raised his hand and swung it down toward her in a long powerful swing aimed at her head. Jammed between Jeremy and Slade, she couldn't duck the blow.

Slade moved his shoulder just a little so he was in front of her. Even though he was bigger, the blow rocked him back on his heels. Slade grunted with the force of it.

Susan just stood. The servant turned his attention to Slade.

Pendleton poked Slade in the chest. "Now you, big fella." Slade was big, but the servant was bigger. Slade began to hurriedly empty his pockets. He sniffed loudly, but his hands never hesitated as all his treasures tumbled out onto the table.

Susan looked at him closely. There was a large red mark on the side of his head where the blow had landed.

Slade started on his trouser pockets. His treasures tumbled onto the table: brooches he had stolen from passengers, a whistle from an officer, a wooden top he'd taken from a child, and—Susan's crystal.

Susan saw only her crystal. Her hand darted out toward it.

Bang. Pendleton hit her hard across her reaching hand. He had picked up a stick that had been leaning against the table.

"Oh, please do that again," Pendleton sniggered. "I do like using my stick." And he waved the stick in her face.

Susan's hand was on fire. Tears sprung to her eyes.

While she tried to work the sting from her fingers, all three were bundled through the barred door, and it slammed shut behind them.

Pendleton picked through the treasures on the table and, chuckling to himself, pocketed a brooch and the whistle. His stubby, dirty fingers passed right over the crystal and did not pick it up. He left the lantern burning on the table when he climbed back up the stairs so they had a little light to see by.

By the time his footsteps had faded, a circle of pale faces had surrounded Susan, Jeremy, and Slade.

Small, cold hands took Susan's injured hand and gently patted it. It hurt, but in some way, the gesture comforted her. Jeremy spoke first.

"What is this place?" he asked. "Where are we, and why are we here?"

Susan heard a collective sigh, as though every boy in that crowded room had been holding his breath. Thin, cold hands pulled her down to sit on the floor. Jeremy sat next to her, and surprisingly enough, Slade sat very close, too. *He's very quiet,* Susan thought.

"My name is Bretton," one of the boys spoke up.

He moved to stand in front of them. Susan saw a boy of about her age and height. His face was thin and pinched. His hair was long and dirty. Floppy curls hung in his eyes. His clothes were even more ragged than Jeremy's. His arms stuck out of his shirtsleeve about three inches.

"We live here," Bretton continued. "This is where orphans come off the ships, and we have to work very hard for Mr. Brinkley, and he looks after us."

"Is this how he looks after us?" Susan couldn't help asking. "Keeping us in a cold, damp basement, locked in a room."

Again she heard the sigh, and many hands reached out of the dark to silently pat her shoulder.

Gradually over the next little while, the story came out. Some of the smaller boys nodded off to sleep with their heads resting on the knees of the older boys. Everyone in the room was an orphan. All had arrived in New York by ship. All their parents had died on the voyage from England. All had been taken prisoner just before landing and brought to this place.

Every day they were forced to work in a large room upstairs. They sewed grain sacks and leather goods for Mr. Brinkley. At the end of their work day, they were herded back into the basement, where they stayed until it was light enough to work again. They were all hungry, cold, and tired. Some had fallen ill and died.

With the story told, the boys sat quietly together. What was there to say? Susan had a million questions, but the words would not take form.

After a little while, Bretton stirred.

"We must all get some sleep now." He lifted the small boy who had fallen asleep in his lap. "We have to work hard tomorrow, or we will be beaten." He laid the limp little figure on a cot.

Jeremy hauled Susan—Samuel—to her feet, and they stumbled through the cots until they found empty ones together. Slade followed them.

"Why did you let the servant hit you?" Susan looked closely at Slade.

He looked down at his shoes. "You saved me on the stairs." Slade looked up at them. "The servant said I was lucky to have friends. You saved me." His face looked a lot softer. "It's a long time since anyone did anything for me."

"What about all those boys you hung around with on the ship?" Susan scoffed.

Slade shrugged. "They were more afraid of me, I think. None of them came looking to see what had happened to me. They left the ship without looking for me. You two saved me on the stairs, and you didn't have to, but you did it anyway."

Slade looked off into a corner. "I had a family once," he said quietly. "They died. I was very young. Sent to the workhouse, I was. Beatings was what you got. Work harder, beating. Beaten for your food – and your sleeping space and your clothes and sometimes, just because." Slade shrugged. "I learned to beat too. Ran away from the place, I did. Hung around Covent Gardens in London. Could get food there. Slade they called me. Took stuff. Coppers after me. Shipped out for America." Slade stopped talking. Shook his head.

Susan and Jeremy looked at each other. What could they say?

"We better get some sleep," Jeremy murmured. "Tomorrow is going to be another nasty day for us, I think."

The three lay down on cots and tried to sleep. Soon Slade's breathing took on an even tempo. *Sleep*, Susan thought. *Mum and Dad must be worried sick.*

Jeremy tugged at her sleeve. He put his fingers to his lips, and the two of them tiptoed to the barred door.

"Susan, we have to keep it a secret that you're a girl." Jeremy stood very close and whispered in her ear. She could feel his breath tickling the wispy hair near her ear.

"If only we could escape from here," she whispered in response. "We could make our own way." Lying on the table, her crystal flashed in the lamplight. Susan's attention was immediately caught.

If only I was still the Guardian of the crystal, she thought wistfully, *I could rescue everyone somehow.*

Jeremy's eyes followed hers until he, too, was staring at the crystal. There it sat on the table, surrounded by the other treasures from Slade's pocket.

It was all too much for Susan. She missed her home, her mum, her dad, even Judy. She was in a stinky basement, pretending to be a boy. She was hungry, cold, tired, and she needed a shower, and none of it was her fault.

I want the crystal, she thought fiercely. *I want it.*

Jeremy clutched her arm; he was still staring at the crystal. "Susan, your crystal just moved on the table," he whispered urgently.

"Did it?" Susan was puzzled. She stared hard, and it did seem to be in a different place. "Now what could have caused it to move?"

Wait, Susan remembered. *I was wanting the crystal. It's worth a try,* she thought. She stretched her hand out toward the crystal. *You're mine,* she thought at the crystal.

"It seemed to move," Jeremy whispered.

You're mine, crystal, and I want you in my hand right now, Susan thought loudly—if you can think of thoughts as loud.

The crystal winked in the lamplight. It moved; it scraped along the table. It hesitated and wobbled on the very edge, sending flashes of light onto the walls. And then true and straight and more immediately than anyone could notice, the crystal was nestled in Susan's clasping hand.

Susan turned to Jeremy in triumph. *I've always had the power to summon it. I've learned something here.* She screwed up her face. *All that time in Slade's pocket. I thought I'd lost it. I doubted. I shouldn't have doubted. I am the Guardian of the crystal like Mrs. Coleman said.*

"I'll be back soon, Jeremy," she whispered. "I'll bring food for everyone."

Jeremy held her fast.

"Susan, don't come back." He shook his head. "Save yourself," he went on. "You saved me on the ship, and I'm in America now, and I thank you. I can make my own way." He took her by the shoulders and looked solemnly into her eyes. "Don't come back," he said. "I don't want you in any more danger."

"Nonsense, I'll be back in the morning." Susan pulled on her jacket. She thought hard about her bedroom, her bed, and vanished from New York and appeared in her bedroom at home. Even in a mess it looked good to her.

She took a deep breath. The air smelled fresh and clean with a slight whiff of laundry soap. Susan let out a huge sigh. Home. Her stomach rumbled. Hungry. Susan crept quickly downstairs to the fridge.

■ ■ ■

While she wolfed into a huge, overflowing sandwich, her eyes strayed to the garbage bags neatly tied by the back door. They stood there, ready to be put out for the garbage truck in the morning.

Susan gulped hard. Yesterday should have been garbage day—the day she spent on the ship.

She used her fingers to try to get it straight. She was on the ship for a night, and then a day, and then spent most of the next night at the orphanage. It should be the day after garbage day. Susan smiled. This was perfect. She arrived home only moments after she left. The time she was away was different time somehow.

That means I can get some sleep and prepare before I have to rush back to Jeremy. Susan sighed with relief.

Quietly she tiptoed upstairs and curled into her wonderful bed.

21

SUSAN'S CRYSTAL

When Susan opened her eyes the next morning, her first thought was of the crystal. She found it quickly because it was clasped tightly in her hand. She climbed out of bed, placed the crystal carefully on the dresser, and walked over to the wardrobe. Turning, she held out her hand and staring hard at the crystal, willed it to come to her. And there it was, tight in her palm.

Next, she put it on the windowsill and shut the window. Then she turned around three times and, with her eyes tight shut, willed the crystal to come to her. "Ow." The crystal hit her knuckles and came to rest on the back of her hand.

"You really are mine." Susan laughed. Tossing the crystal up in the air and catching it, she slipped it into her pocket and started downstairs for breakfast.

Breakfast. Mum and Dad. She hoped she was right in her theory. Arriving home moments after she had left would be very useful. *There'd be a lot less explaining to do,* she thought.

Down the stairs she went. She felt so different she was sure they would notice.

Dad was polishing his shoes with the tin of shoe polish balanced on his knee. Mum was standing over the sink, dabbing at a spot on her blouse.

"Good morning, Susan," she said, rubbing harder. "Can you remember what gets strawberry jam out of cotton?"

"Good morning, Mum." Susan kissed her cheek. "Sorry, can't remember." It all seemed so normal.

The newspaper lay on the table, and as Susan went over to peck her dad on the cheek, she noticed the date. It was the next morning; she'd been right. *I can control it,* she realized. *I think myself to the time I want.* The time she had been away was like no time. She slipped her hand into her pocket to feel the crystal. It was warm to the touch.

She busied herself making toast.

Mum now had a wet patch on the front of her blouse, but the stain was gone. She poured herself another coffee and brought it over to the table. Dad dropped his shoe to the floor and started on the second one.

Susan went to the cupboard for the peanut butter. Her hand reached out for the doorknob, but she stopped short. The notice board attached to the cupboard door had one name scrawled across it in her mother's hasty writing. It said: *Miranda Coleman, 4:00 p.m.*

Susan dropped her butter knife with a clatter.

Her mother saw where she was looking.

"Oh yes, Susan," she said, putting her plate in the dish-washer. "A lady called for you. She said it was something about a crystal she gave you." Susan's mum fluttered her hand in the air. "Something about a terrible mistake. She's coming at four this afternoon to pick it up."

Seeing the look on Susan's face, her mother frowned "That is all right with you, isn't it?"

Susan swallowed hard. "Yes, sure, she's a nice lady." She didn't know what to say.

"Oh good, because I forgot to get her phone number to call her back if it wasn't OK, so I was hoping it would be all right with you." Susan's mother bent and kissed her head.

"Peow, Susan, your hair smells terrible. You really need to wash it. What have you been doing?"

"I don't know," Susan stammered. How do you tell your mother you spent one night in the freezing cold on the open deck of a stinking ship and the next in the cellar of a boys' orphanage?

You don't.

"I'll go shower straight away."

She headed for the stairs, but then came back to where her mum was gathering together her sketches to take to her studio out back.

"I love you, Mum," she said and pecked her on the cheek.

"Ho, and what about me, Suzie Loon Tune?" Her dad stood up and held his arms wide.

Susan rushed to him and gave him a big hug.

"Yes, you, too." She laughed. "I'm very lucky to have you two." And then Susan ran upstairs for a shower.

■ ■ ■

As she dressed she began making plans. It was obvious to her that Mrs. Coleman was going to correct her mistake by taking back the crystal. Just when she had become used to it and was beginning to get it to work properly for her. *I was beginning to think of it as mine*, she thought.

I'll save Jeremy first, she thought as she brushed her hair out. She was about to fluff it up with her hands, but...*it will look more boyish if I keep it straight back*. So she brushed it hard down against her head.

She pulled out a pair of jeans and boots and looked around for the most boyish sweatshirt she could find. They all had pictures printed on the front, but she found a dark green one and turned it inside out. Now for a coat for her, and another one for Jeremy.

After grabbing her knapsack from the mudroom, she stuffed in all the apples from the fruit bowl. There were a couple of oranges; they went in, too.

While digging for trail mix in the cupboard above the sink, she spotted a box pushed to the back. The word *tea* sprang out at her, and she grabbed the box. Quickly she opened it and found black leaves, all twisted and dry, just like Jeremy had described. The box was full. The label said Assam's Finest Loose Tea.

I'm sure this will help Jeremy, Susan thought with satisfaction as she shoved the box into her pack. She grabbed the cookies. In they went. Susan was ready.

Taking the crystal out of her pocket, she wondered what should happen next.

I hope I arrive early enough, she thought.

Then she remembered the crystal belonged to her. *I can decide where to go and when to arrive*, she realized. *I'll go to Jeremy.*

Carefully, she formed a picture of him in her mind. Then she built the picture to include his surroundings as she remembered them. Finally she stared at her crystal and asked it to take her there.

The sliding, the smearing, the colors slipping sideways, and she was there.

■ ■ ■

Susan reached down, confident that her crystal would have landed her near Jeremy. She fumbled till she found his shoulder.

"Jeremy, it's me, wake up," she whispered, shaking him gently.

Bretton sat up from across the lines of cots. He was more attuned to sounds in the night.

"What's happening?" he wanted to know. Bretton came straight to his feet and quickly stepped across the cots.

"Shhhhhhhh." Susan started the hushing, but Jeremy joined in, awake now.

Susan pulled Bretton down so their three heads were very close together.

"I'm going to rescue you," she murmured.

Bretton just looked in blank disbelief. "I've wracked me brain trying to get away, Samuel," he said. "I even tried a couple of times." He shook his head. "The door is iron. None of us is small enough to fit through the bars, particularly you, Samuel."

Susan smiled to herself. "Just get everyone ready to leave," she said. "I think it's time we all left this place."

Jeremy smiled, but Bretton shook his head. "But how?"

"You leave that to me." Susan stood, pulled her parka straight with a determined jerk, and groped for her crystal. Her crystal. She smiled at the thought and then disappeared—completely.

22

ESCAPE

Susan popped back to her bedroom and then straight back to the courtyard where she had seen the sign.

I'm getting the hang of this, she thought happily.

She hugged the courtyard wall in the dark. Only one window showed a light. Hardly daring to breathe, she crept along the wall until she could peep in.

She looked into the kitchen. A skinny young girl wearily tipped water into a large saucepan set out on the woodstove. Susan saw flames in the window of the stove. The servant girl was sweating in the heat. *She looks as miserable and tired as the boys,* Susan thought. *I wonder if she's an orphan, too.* The girl threw in a few scoops of oats and stood there, stirring with a long wooden spoon. She yawned and her head nodded, but she kept stirring.

Breakfast, thought Susan, shrugging her pack closer onto her back and thinking of the food it contained.

The clock on the wall to the side of the stove said half past three. The girl, finished with her stirring, sat down next to a guttering candle and took up a shirt she was mending. As Susan watched, the tired girl leaned forward over her work and rested her head on the table. Very soon she was fast asleep.

Susan could see the doorway down to the basement through the kitchen window. She tried the door to the kitchen, but it was locked.

Taking a deep breath, Susan began very gently to lift the window. It slid easily. It didn't make a sound. Susan climbed over the sill and stood in the shadows away from the flickering candle.

Remember to keep breathing, she thought, and took a long, soft breath. *I hope my knees aren't making as much noise as my heart.* Susan searched the walls, hoping to see a key to the basement.

Susan moved her hands carefully around the door frame, hoping people in old New York kept the key by the door. She made her fingers brush the wall lightly and silently, all her concentration focused on her fingertips. None of her attention was on her knees, though; her knee scraped against an empty bucket. It clattered to the floor before she could catch it.

The girl at the table sat bolt upright with a squeal.

"I wasn't asleep really," she stammered even before she turned and saw Susan frozen by the basement door. In a moment, her expression changed from shrinking fear to anger.

"What are you out of the cellar for?" she demanded. "Breakfast isn't done yet." She moved menacingly toward Susan.

"I'll catch it if you're found up here," the girl worried. As she came closer, she caught at a bunch of keys, swinging from her belt.

"I'll get a beating. You'll get no breakfast." She grabbed at Susan's arm. "You'll be sorry. I don't need no trouble."

Susan was about to fight her. She wanted to strike out, but at the last moment, she remembered from her classes to use her foes' strengths against them. So she stood. Still.

The drab squeezed her arm hard. Tears of anger and pain started to Susan's eyes. She bit her lip and waited.

With her spare hand, the servant girl groped the correct key and pushed it hard into the lock. She kept a firm hold on Susan's arm.

The key turned, the girl pushed on the latch, and the door swung open. Susan went completely limp. She dropped to the floor of the landing, and the unexpectedness of her action forced the girl to topple over into the corridor. Susan was up in a flash and shut the door, trapping the servant girl.

Susan grabbed her arm and hauled her down the stairs. The girl struggled and swung around to hit out at Susan.

"Sshhhhhhhh." Shushing noises came from below. Everyone was up and dressed. Susan pulled at the keys hanging from the girl's belt. Susan dragged the girl, who was groaning and crying, over closer to the barred door and started trying the keys in the lock.

The first one fit the lock—but it wouldn't turn.

Susan pushed the girl up against the door and leaned her weight on her to keep her still. "I'll be beaten." The girl was crying hard now. "They'll blame me, they will."

The second key wouldn't even fit into the keyhole.

The boys gathered on the other side of the bars. She saw their pale faces in the dim lantern light. She heard rustlings and murmurs, but nobody spoke. Susan knew there had been noise and it was close to dawn.

Susan tried a third key, but in trying to get it into the lock, she fumbled the bunch and they all fell back together. She would have to start again.

The servant girl groped her hand free and pointed to the bunch. "Will you take me with you?" Susan pushed harder and started again. The key would not go in the lock.

The girl started to wriggle. "Can someone on your side of the bars hold her for me?" Susan whispered.

Jeremy was there, and so was Bretton.

"That's Violet," Bretton murmured. "She's all right."

"She nearly took my arm off upstairs," Susan whispered back. "Hold her someone."

Jeremy stretched his arms through and grabbed the struggling Violet, leaving Susan with both hands free to work on the keys.

But Violet gave a desperate wriggle and pulled free of Jeremy's hands; she jumped back, pulling the keys from Susan's grasp.

Susan gathered herself to spring up the steps after Violet, but Violet wasn't running; she was standing, smoothing her skirts. Then she reached down and picked one key from the bunch and held it out.

"This key." She sniffed, wiping her eyes.

Susan took it and tried it in the lock. It worked. The door swung open.

"Samuel, I wouldn't have believed it." Bretton was the first out the door. "We are rescued." Bretton was first up the stairs, going as quietly as he could. The others followed. The larger boys carried the smaller.

One small boy tugged on Violet's skirt as they filed passed, and she bent and picked him up. Then Violet joined the group moving quietly up the stairs.

Susan and Jeremy were the last out.

"Do you think she's safe?" Susan wanted to know.

Jeremy nodded. "I don't think she can stay if we get away."

Jeremy looked ahead to Violet, helping with some of the smaller children.

"She very thin and probably gets beaten. It looked like a bruise on her arm, and Bretton said she was all right."

Susan craned her head back into the dormitory. "There's someone still sleeping back there."

"Yes, it's Slade." Jeremy pulled on her arm. "Leave him."

But Susan dug her heels in. "We can't leave anyone in this horrible place."

Jeremy fingered his eye, which was still tender. "Come on, we need to go."

Susan shook her head. "No, I can't leave him here. He took a hit for me from Pendleton. He isn't all bad."

"He isn't all good, either," Jeremy grumped.

But Susan was sure she was right. "Jeremy, you go ahead. I'll get Slade. We'll be right behind you."

Jeremy shrugged. "I guess you're right. I'll help you wake him up."

Very quickly the two of them hurried back through the cots and over to where Slade slept.

Jeremy grabbed his shoulder and gave him a rough shake. "Get up, get up." He flicked Slade's ear.

"Huh, huh." Slade woke, swinging his arms and flailing about.

"Sssshhhhhh," Susan and Jeremy hissed. And Slade was quiet. Just his eyes moving from one to the other.

Jeremy grabbed his blanket and pulled. Susan made beckoning motions. After a quick look around at the empty cots, Slade leaped up.

When Susan and Jeremy headed for the open door, he followed close behind.

Susan stopped at the table and gathered up all the scattered treasures there. With a quick smile, she handed Jeremy the small stone he had brought from home.

The trio tiptoed up the stairs together. Quietly, quietly.

23

WHERE TO?

They found the others huddled against the wall in the courtyard.

"Where will we go?" one of the younger children asked.

Bretton looked as though he had just realized that escaping from the basement was the beginning of their adventure instead of the end.

All eyes turned to Susan.

She looked around desperately. She didn't know what to do. Her eyes fell on the sign she had glimpsed earlier. She hurried over to it and in the first dim light of the coming dawn read the whole sign.

Rescue home for orphan boys.
Welcome, orphan dears. Find shelter here with us.
We, the people of New York, have made this
home for you so you may prosper in your new
land. Here you will learn to read and write and
the art of sums so you may earn an honest
living in this great new land.
Mrs. Horace Blackwood
Chairwoman and Founding Member
Orphan Benevolent Society.

"We'll go see her," Susan said, and she pointed to the sign.

But Jeremy only looked puzzled, and the others gathered round and they looked puzzled, too. *They probably can't read.* In a hurried whisper, she read the notice to the gathered children.

Susan thought the children would immediately realize that they had been wrongly treated, but when she finished reading, there was total silence.

All eyes were on the sign, and many of the mouths were open.

Finally Bretton shook his head in wonder. "Often Mr. Brinkley read the sign to us. When he read, it said we were to work hard and never complain and to take our beatings bravely so we would grow to be men."

"He tricked you," Jeremy said, picking up a small child and settling him on his hip. "Come, let's get out of here before they catch us."

With nods the children all moved across the courtyard to the gate.

Violet had a key.

Outside they hurried silently along in a straggling line.

New York. Susan thought of the television shows she had seen of New York. Skyscrapers, millions of people, cars, buses, street vendors, rock concerts in the park.

The New York Susan hurried through with the children was like a small country town. No apartment buildings at all. Most buildings were just little houses. *They look handmade. They look like sheds*, Susan thought.

Each seemed to have a large yard, and Susan could see chickens and goats and occasionally a cow as they hurried along. The road was a muddy track, and the sidewalk was just a foot path.

There were people about, though, working in their yards and walking along the pathways. Susan was at the end of the straggly line of children and saw that many people watched the children with interest. They were a very conspicuous group, so many raggedy children out without an adult. Only Slade and Violet looked even remotely grown up.

Susan moved up beside Jeremy and leaned over to whisper in his ear.

"We must get these children somewhere to hide. We stick out too much all together on the street. Just a couple of us should go to visit Mrs. Blackwood."

Jeremy turned his worried face to her.

"How will we find this Mrs. Blackwood, do you think? That's a very large city over there." Jeremy waved his hand to where they could see many, many buildings jammed together.

"It looks like we're on the edge of it." Susan waved at their surroundings. "This looks almost like country to me."

"We should head toward the part of town where the rich people live for a start," Susan said after thinking for a bit. "But we must get this group hidden before too many people are out on the streets. Mr. Brinkley could find us by just asking."

"They'll start looking for us soon," Violet said, coming up to them. "The porridge will be burning by now, and that'll wake 'em up."

"Some of the younger ones are getting hungry, too." Bretton joined them as they hurried along.

"I have food in my pack."

"There's a copse where we can hide." Jeremy pointed off to the side where a small group of trees stood in a field. Sheep grazed on the short grass.

Some of the children climbed over the fence; some smaller ones squeezed through. Susan was surprised to see Slade lifting some of the small children over. Soon they were all safely hidden in among the trees.

While Violet distributed the trail mix to the children, Susan walked over to where Slade was sitting by himself. "Thank you for helping with the smaller children."

Slade looked up, surprised. "They needed help," he said.

Susan shook her head. "You've changed so much."

Slade shrugged. "You made me remember when I had a family, brothers, and sisters. It was nice."

"Well, you can have it again with these children. They need your help, right now."

Slade looked up at Susan under his eyelashes. "I'd like to give you a gift for helping me." Then he shrugged. "But I don't have anything now." He looked up suddenly. "I have one thing. One thing I've kept secret since my family all died," he said. "My name, my name is…" He hesitated. "My name is Rupert," he said in a rush. Then put his head down.

Susan just looked at him. How people can surprise you.

She took a deep breath. "Thank you…Rupert," she said. "Thank you for telling me your secret." She put her hand on his shoulder for a moment and then walked back to where Bretton and Jeremy were waiting.

"This isn't how I thought New York would be," Susan said.

Violet nodded. "Brinkley didn't want the children too near the city. He needed to be out here so that the charity ladies wouldn't see what he was doing and how he was keeping the boys." She waved her hand to the east. "Most of the city is over there on a big island called Manhattan."

A little boy came up to the group. He tugged at Bretton's sleeve.

"What is it, Hector?" Bretton knelt beside the boy.

Hector held out a dirty piece of paper. "I'm cold," he said. "I found this paper. Can we light a fire?"

"Good idea, Hector," Bretton said. "Let's do that."

"Wait!" Susan reached for the paper. "Look, it's a newspaper. We can learn stuff from this." She began to read. The others looked on.

Slade joined the group. "It's only a dirty piece of paper. What can it tell you?"

"Lots." Susan looked up, smiling. "Here, see," she said, pointing at the top. "This is the *New York Daily Mail.*"

"So?" Bretton shrugged.

"Look. Here. The paper is published by Mr. Horace Blackwood." Susan waved the paper above her head. "Mr. Horace Blackwood," she crowed.

Bretton, Violet, Slade, and Jeremy exchanged puzzled glances.

Jeremy frowned. "But, Susan—"

Susan interrupted him. "The name of the woman on the wall at the orphanage was Mrs. Horace Blackwood."

The others still looked puzzled.

"We can find the newspaper place easily, and that can lead us to the lady," Susan explained.

Jeremy leaned over the paper and peered at it. "Does it say where he lives?"

"I bet the paper comes from that place Violet mentioned." Bretton waved toward Manhattan.

"Just a couple of us should go to this lady and explain the situation," Susan said. "But who?"

"Bretton of course, and Susan. She can read," Jeremy suggested.

"Susan?"

"Samuel?" Bretton asked

"Susan actually," she said, nodding. "We didn't want Mr. Brinkley to split us up."

"It has to be two boys. It was a boy's orphanage."

"That makes sense."

Susan nodded. "Jeremy, you and Bretton go to find Mrs. Blackwood. Just keep asking people, very politely, where the paper comes from. Take this copy with you. Slade can protect the children, and Violet can help look after them."

They all nodded, willing to take her suggestions as orders.

"I'll go get more food," she added.

"How will you do that?" Slade wanted to know.

"Oh, I have my ways." Susan grinned. "I'll be back as soon as I can."

She picked up her pack and moved off through the trees. She didn't want them to see her disappear in a poof.

"Wait, Susan." Jeremy followed her.

She slowed to let him catch up.

"How can I ever thank you for all your help?"

Susan was surprised. Yes, she realized, she had helped a lot.

"You know, Jeremy, I enjoyed doing it."

"You enjoyed shivering in a storm on an icy deck and being stuck in a basement with a barred door to keep you in?"

Susan thought a moment. "No, I didn't enjoy those parts, but I enjoyed meeting you. I feel as though we are good friends. I know you better than anyone else."

Jeremy reached down into his pocket. He held out his stone to Susan. "I want you to have this," he said.

"Jeremy, the stone is all you brought from England." Susan's face flushed with pleasure.

Jeremy thrust it into her hand. "I have my knife, and I want this little part of me to be with you."

"Thank you," Susan said, putting the stone into her pocket. "I'll keep it safe." *Maybe I'll collect a stone from every crystal journey I take*, she thought.

Then she remembered. "I brought you some loose tea," she said, and pulled the box out of a different pocket of her pack.

Jeremy took the box from her with trembling hands. "It's such a lot," he said. "This must be very valuable."

"I hope so," Susan said. "It didn't cost very much in my time, though."

Jeremy opened the lid and poured a little out onto his hand. He sniffed the aroma of the tea appreciatively.

"Keep it safe," Susan said. "I'll be back soon."

Jeremy looked up. His eyes were bright and smiling, too.

"I would always want to be your friend, Susan."

"You are, Jeremy. You are my best friend—the best friend I've ever had. You believed me when I told you about the crystal."

At the mention of the crystal, Susan began to feel the familiar sensation of colors blurring and smearing, which meant she was about to travel.

"Oh dear, I didn't start this." Her head was spinning. "Jeremy, I'm going. I don't know why. I didn't start it, but I'm going. I'll try to come back. Good-bye," she called as everything in her universe tore and slipped. When the colors righted themselves again, she was home, in her bedroom.

24

MIRANDA COLEMAN

"There you are, Susan." It was her mother. "I've been looking everywhere for you."

Susan slipped quickly out of her pack.

"Sorry, I didn't hear you call, Mum."

But her mother had just gone right on talking. "Mrs. Coleman is downstairs to see you. Remember, I told you she was coming—didn't I?"

Miranda Coleman. Susan had forgotten about the note on the kitchen notice board. Just when she seemed to have the hang of the crystal and she was starting to enjoy helping people, here was Mrs. Coleman. *She's probably come to take it away because I yelled at her,* Susan thought. She thrust the crystal deep into her pocket. It felt tingly on her leg.

You're mine, she thought at it as she hurried downstairs.

Miranda Coleman sat in the swing chair under the maple tree. She was looking out across the valley, and so Susan saw her before she saw Susan. She looked very peaceful sitting there with her feet gently pushing against the ground to keep the chair swinging.

Susan remembered how rude she had been last time they met at the flea market and wondered if she would ever learn to curb her temper.

Then her foot crunched on the gravel of the path, and Mrs. Coleman turned around. They were facing each other.

"I'm sorry."

They both blurted out the same words at the same time. Then there was silence. Then they laughed together in relief, and Susan ran forward and jumped onto the other end of the swing chair, making it rock wildly.

The two looked at each other, the young and the old. Susan saw an old woman, her skin was wrinkled and her chin was small, but her eyes. Miranda Coleman's eyes were alive and bright. There was humor there, and understanding. *I would like to be like this woman,* Susan realized, and a big grin spread across her face.

"I see your adventure has been going well," said Mrs. Coleman, patting Susan's arm.

"Um." Susan nodded. "Did you pull me back for this meeting? I was in the middle of talking, and all of a sudden, I was pulled back here. Did you do that?"

"Already." Mrs. Coleman nodded approval. "You have done very well then."

"I've tried," Susan acknowledged, "but it isn't finished yet. There is still so much more help I can give."

"You've done enough, I think," Mrs. Coleman said.

And then getting up, she suggested, "Let's walk."

Susan followed her.

"You see," Mrs. Coleman began as they walked down the path to the gate, "if you are sucked back like that, without wanting to, it usually means that you have helped enough and the person will then be able to get along by themselves."

"But Jeremy's my friend. I want to be sure he's OK." Susan picked up a stick and whacked at the heads of the grass stalks alongside the path.

"There can be such a thing as too much help, Susan." Mrs. Coleman glanced at Susan as they walked. "People need to feel that they have control of their own lives and decisions."

Susan whacked the head off a daisy.

"There will be other adventures for you."

"But—"

"There will be—and other friends. You'll see."

"Well, what happens now?"

"The crystal is totally yours now. I can't feel its pull at all anymore. You are the new Guardian of the Crystal."

Susan just kept whacking away at the grass heads. She tried to imagine what it would feel like—or not feel like to have the crystal gone.

"Do you miss it?" she asked in the end.

"Very much." Mrs. Coleman sighed. "It was part of me my whole life. That's why I got so angry at the flea market. It was such a wonderful thing you had, and you didn't seem to want it."

"I shouldn't have been so rude."

"Wait a minute, I'm the adult here. It was for me to be sensible and not get angry." Mrs. Coleman turned to face Susan on the path. She searched for words for a minute. "But already the crystal was so yours, and you didn't even know how wonderful it was, and when I let the crystal draw me onto the ship with you, I could already feel it would be my last Crystal Journey, and I felt so sad." She shook her head. "The crystal has been a large part of my life."

"But there's so much I don't know about how it works. Please, tell me all about it."

Mrs. Coleman shook her head again and smiled. "You must learn for yourself. I think it's different for everybody, and you are already well able to control it—as much as anyone can."

"What do you mean—as much as anyone can?"

They had arrived at the gate, and Mrs. Coleman leaned against it.

"The crystal has a mind of its own, you know." Her eyes had become dreamy, and she was staring off into the trees across the road. "You're the Guardian of the crystal, not the owner of it."

"Like, you mean how it pulled me back this afternoon?" Susan asked.

Mrs. Coleman nodded. "I remember once clutching the crystal in my hand, screaming to be taken home, just screaming—and nothing happened."

Susan's eyes were glued to Mrs. Coleman's face. "What did you do?"

"Oh." Mrs. Coleman focused on Susan with a start. "The reindeer herd just kept rushing toward me. I stood there. I couldn't run; I was up to my knees in snow."

"What happened?" Susan whispered.

Mrs. Coleman laughed. "It must have been the screaming I was doing, I guess, because when the reindeer herd reached me, they split in two and thundered by on either side."

Susan let her breath out slowly. She hadn't realized she was holding it.

"What about time, though? I spent a day and two nights in the past, and when I came back, it was the same night I left."

"Oh, yes, you will get better at returning to the correct time." Mrs. Coleman nodded, smiling. "I almost missed my wedding, but the crystal got me back just in time." She shook her head, smiling and remembering. "I figure I've lived about sixteen years in the past, over and above the time I've had here in the present."

Susan's mouth hung open.

Mrs. Coleman patted her shoulder. "Don't worry about it. It all works out." Then she stepped through the gate and over to her car.

"I have to give you this." Mrs. Coleman reached into her big bag and groped around, peering in.

Susan stretched over and tried to look inside as well. She could see all sorts of things, and Mrs. Coleman's hand revolved them all. A first aid kit came to the surface, and then a huge Swiss army knife, next a woolly scarf—all jumbled together.

"Ah, here it is." Mrs. Coleman pulled out a large envelope. She noticed the bemused expression on Susan's face and laughed.

"You need a bag like this to carry what you will need to have with you. A bag like this is less conspicuous than a pack. A rip stop nylon pack doesn't blend in in most of the places you will go."

Impulsively, she thrust the bag into Susan's hands.

"Here," she said, "this will get you started. Take it with you on your journeys. Now I must go."

Quickly, she hugged Susan, clasping her hard.

"I know you will do very well," she whispered in Susan's ear.

Susan didn't know what to say. Mrs. Coleman was hurrying around to the driver's side of her car.

"Wait," Susan called, holding out the envelope. "What's this?"

"It belongs with the crystal," Mrs. Coleman said, opening the door. "Read it as soon as you can, but keep it secret and don't show anyone."

"But will I see you again?"

"Maybe. I'm not sure. Phone if you need me. My number is on the envelope."

And so saying Mrs. Coleman jumped into her car and drove quickly away.

Susan stood watching until the dust of her passing had settled back onto the road. Then she turned up the path and walked back to the house. She thrust the envelope deep into the bag. *I'll need to find a good hiding place for this,* she thought as she climbed the steps of the porch.

Just then her mother came out through the screen door, carrying a tray with a pot of tea and cookies on a plate.

"Has the lady gone?"

"Yes, she couldn't stay long."

"How funny she was," her mother said, turning and going back inside. "She hardly stayed any time at all, and I wanted to show her my carvings while she was here. What an odd woman..."

Susan could hear her mother muttering all the way back into the kitchen.

Susan hurried up to her room. She was just reaching for the envelope when she heard her mother coming up the stairs.

Susan thrust the envelope back into Mrs. Coleman's bag and shoved it under her bed as her mother reached the landing. She carried a brown paper bag.

"I found the tin for the library display. I dug it out this morning. So now that the lady has gone, we can take it in. I need to go to the supermarket, all the fruit and cookies seem to have vanished." Susan's mother shook her head. "You can take the tin to the library for me," Susan's mother said.

25

FARADAY'S TEAS

Susan's mum dropped her off at the library, and Susan went inside. Her body was walking, carrying the bag with the tin in it. Susan even held the door for a man leaving the library with his arms loaded high with books. Her brain, though, was with Jeremy, how she would never see him again and never find out what happened to him.

Margaret stood behind the desk, checking out books. Susan just stood there with the brown paper bag in her hand. Margaret came over as soon as she finished with the borrower.

"I brought the extra tin Mum promised." Susan thrust the bag into Margaret's hands. She turned to leave, but friendly Margaret put her hand on her shoulder and steered her toward the display.

"Come and see; now it's finished."

The display looked good. The ship sitting so still in its glass case looked nothing like the ship Susan had been on, bucking and tossing on every wave. The library was silent compared with the constant hiss of the waves, the whining wind, and the chatter of the children. And the smell. Susan leaned closer to the little ship. She could almost smell the tar and dirty laundry, with the salt tang over all.

"Hey, this is great! A Faraday tin." Margaret was holding Susan's tea tin in her hands.

"You know, this person arrived in New York as an orphan but got into the tea trade. Nobody knows where he got his first lot of tea, but he sold it and used the money to invest in more tea. He sailed on the clippers…"

Susan snatched the tin from her hands.

"…and became very rich, sailing tea from India."

Susan stared at the picture on the side of the tin.

"It's funny, you know, but it was always a rule in the Faraday Company: his picture on every tin," Margaret continued.

"His picture and his knife," Susan murmured. She was staring at a picture of Jeremy, grandly dressed and holding out his knife. She knew it was Jeremy by the way his smile showed in his eyes. And she could plainly see the whale carved into the bone knife handle.

Margaret had grown quiet and was watching Susan closely.

Susan rubbed her thumb over the picture. So Jeremy was safe and had done well, and he'd sent her a message through the years.

She was happy for him but sad for herself. She knew, now, she would never see him again.

Margaret gently took the tin from her hands.

"Thanks for bringing it in, Susan. This is a great addition to the display." She placed Jeremy's tin with the other one and stood back to admire her work.

"Do you have a book with his story in it?" Susan asked.

Margaret looked up with a smile.

"Susan, you're full of good ideas; I believe we do."

Margaret hurried off to the stacks, leaving Susan alone with the tin. Jeremy looked a lot older than when she knew him, but happy and prosperous.

I really did help. Susan smiled to herself. *I'll read the book about Jeremy after the display,* she thought. She patted her pocket and felt the crystal tingle there, as though it answered her thoughts.

She skipped a step as she walked outside to wait for her mum.

Author's Website: **www.grosemaryludlow.com**

Thank you for reading "A Rare Gift". I hope you enjoyed reading about Susan's adventures as much as I enjoyed writing them.

In Book 2 of Susan's Crystal Journals she is drawn to Ancient Egypt with only one very slim chance of ever returning home. Watch for Pharaoh's Tomb which will be available in December 2016.

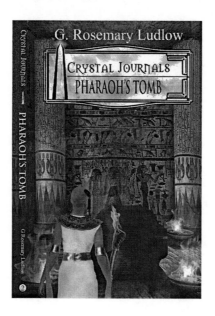

BIOGRAPHY
G. ROSEMARY LUDLOW

G. Rosemary Ludlow is a storyteller who spent years in her native Australia as a schoolteacher. Whether she taught children history, geography, or arithmetic, Rosemary always found a way to integrate stories in the classroom.

After moving to Canada, Rosemary spent time working at a truck factory, a lumber company, and even an aluminum smelter. With her husband she produced and wrote hundreds of video training programs for industry.

Rosemary has maintained her passion for storytelling.

She lives in Vancouver, Canada with her husband. They walk in the wonderful parks around their home.

Rosemary says that her hobbies are reading, knitting and photography.

CPSIA information can be obtained
at www.ICGtesting.com
Printed in the USA
LVOW10s2236041217
558591LV00014B/2022/P